the trouble with us

Trouble series

Book Two

christina c jones

acknowledgements

I would have thought that with each project, these acknowledgements would get easier to write.

They don't, lol.

Even though the group of people around me who make writing possible remains pretty consistent, I still find myself having a hard time coming up with words that convey my thanks enough.

So, I'll keep it simple
Thank You!

To my family, my friends, my readers, and my AWESOME beta readers, MW, LW, CJ, MM, CI, SW, NH, TM, JW, AS, and AM, who volunteer their time to help me insure that my vision for each couple's story is clearly conveyed.

THANK YOU!

one

. . .

bianca

IT STARTED with me minding my own business.

All I wanted to do was have a couple of drinks.

Alone.

Not that I knew anybody anyway, but still. I'd unpacked the last of my boxes, finally had myself settled into my new apartment, and a little music, a little tequila, and a little people watching seemed like the perfect way to end my day. A quick internet search led me to Urban Grind, a cool little hybrid of a coffee shop and lounge, with live music, great bartenders, and a perfect vibe.

Until *they* sat down.

A group of couples collapsed into the booth next to my quiet little table for one, talking, laughing, and sweating off a round on the dance floor. The stage was empty, so I pretended to be absorbed in something on my phone as two of them, a man and a woman, settled into conversation.

"Aiight, one of y'all admit this shit so we can move on, please. Women are *liars*."

"Whatever, Shad. You keep making this claim, but you haven't said anything to back it up. Just stop."

"*Me? I* should stop? Come on, Raisa, you know I'm telling the truth. Women *say* they can do this no strings attached thing, but they *can't*. They *say* they can do the friends with benefits thing, but they *can't*. Women catch feelings, it's in their nature. You tell a woman up front that the only thing you're tryna do with them is the bedroom boom, she agrees with it, and then all of a sudden shit changes. They wanna talk about being in love. I've done enough first hand research to write a study on it. Women can't have sex — not *good* sex — and not fall in love. Impossible."

"That's bullshit."

"So I'm lying? You're saying I'm lying?"

"I'm saying it's bullshit."

"So I don't know what I'm talking about? Okay, let's ask somebody else. Hey, excuse me. What about you? What do *you* think?"

It took me a second to realize that the male end of that conversation, *Shad*, as the woman had called him, was talking to *me*. I looked toward their table, and right into a pair of charismatic eyes, a shade darker than their owner's rich pecan-colored skin.

Oh, damn.

He was *fine*. Even with two tables between us, he exuded confident, magnetic energy that made a shallow tightness pull at my chest. Both his hair and beard were neatly, freshly trimmed, and he gave me an easy, pristine, *sexy* smile that made my chest a little tighter still.

Yeah... women *were* liars.

With a guy who looked like *that*, I had no doubt that he'd dealt with a string of women who swore up and down they were only in it for sex, just to work their way into his bed. Once they got there, they would pull out their little personal bag of tricks. Be a Rihanna in bed, Ina Garten in the kitchen, Michelle Obama in public, and a CeCe Winans for his mama, all so *they* could be the one he saw as *the one*. The *one* who would make him different, make him want to stake his claim and *put a ring on it*.

And then, when he tired of them and was ready to move on, he became the bad guy. All because they weren't listening, because they thought *their* pussy was enchanted enough to *change* him. His experience was valid, and while I certainly couldn't — nor did I have a desire to — deny *that*... it didn't make his generalization any less painfully *wrong*.

If we limited the group to mutual desirability between he and his potential partner, yes, there was a group of women — who he obviously *attracted* — who were exactly what he'd pegged them. They were liars. But then, there was a group who wouldn't touch him with a ten-foot pole, because they were keen enough to recognize him as one of *those* guys, the deliverers of *dick too bomb*. The kind of man who was acutely aware of his appeal, and used it brazenly, to get a woman comfortable enough to let him screw them silly. But *they* weren't silly, so they left guys like "Shad" the hell alone.

And *then*, you have the group that guys like him don't think exist. Women who would make his little toes curl backward, then dodge his desperate two-in-the-morning phone calls, because *they* weren't trying to be locked down.

I could have said all of that in response to his question, but I didn't, because...

You can't tell people you don't believe in love.

Well... wait, let me rephrase: You *shouldn't* tell people you don't believe in love.

Cause as soon as you do, they wanna break you down, figure you out, *get to the root of what makes you so bitter,* as if not buying into love as the pinnacle of relational happiness automatically means you must have endured some type of tragic heartbreak. They get all in your business, and I don't like people in *my* business, so... I kept my mouth shut. I couldn't tell him that I disagreed, because then I would have to explain, and in the course of explaining, I would out myself as a disbeliever in the notion of relationships based on romantic love.

So... yeah.

"I'm sorry, what?" I asked, wrinkling my nose in feigned curiosity. He was seated on the outside edge of the booth, with enough separation between him and the woman next to him to figure that *she* wasn't the other half of his couple. Actually... on further observation, he seemed to be the seventh wheel of the group.

"Don't mind my brother," the woman beside him said, leaning around him so I could see her face. Now that she mentioned the relation, with her face right next to his, I could see the similarities in skin tone and feature. Somehow, they were *equally* gorgeous. With her face pulled into an obviously playful scowl, she swatted him on the arm. "Rashad, leave that girl alone. She doesn't wanna be bothered with you."

Rashad turned his legs out of the booth toward me, and leaned in closer as he spoke over his shoulder. "I'm not *bothering* her, I'm asking her a question. I'm not bothering you, am I?" He directed that query at me with a little smirk, like he just *knew* the answer. *Of course* I wasn't perturbed by him impeding on my one-woman girls night out, because he was *Rashad...* I should be *flattered.*

"Actually... you kinda *are.*" I picked up my Brave Bull, raising the little plastic straw to my mouth to sip on the mixture of tequila and coffee liqueur. His eyebrows hiked up, but his smirk didn't waver. As a matter of fact, the corners of his mouth twitched like he was trying not to let it spread into a *bigger* smile.

Still holding that amused expression, he lifted his hands in conciliation. "My bad then. But since I've already interrupted, I may as well go ahead and ask my question, right?"

Before I could respond, he was already out of his seat, and I had to look up — *way up* — to still be able to see his face. He was wearing dark jeans, a casual dark grey blazer, and a tee shirt in a candy-apple red that looked delicious against his rich skin. Once he was beside me, he knelt down, draping his arm across the back of my chair.

"Now, these crazy-assed people over here," he said, pointing at his friends in the booth, "Are trying to tell me that women can separate sex from emotion, and I don't see it. *I* think they're messing around because it's me. I need an unbiased answer, okay? You're a beautiful woman, I'm sure you've had some grown up relationships... tell me what *you* think."

He turned to me, snaring me with those dark golden-brown eyes as he ran his tongue over his lips. He was close enough that the subtle, leathery scent of his cologne permeated my senses, and the heat from his body radiated onto mine, sending warm tingles over my skin.

Rashad held my gaze with confidence, and it took everything in me not to break into a smile. He was *good.* Very, very good.

"I think," I said, tipping my head to the side, "that you are arrogant, probably a little spoiled, definitely narrow-minded, and... too handsome for your own good."

He chuckled, and I despised the way the earnest sound vibrated in my chest, tugging at me and making me want to join in. "Is that your way of telling me to leave you alone?"

"Smart man." I gave him the barest hint of a smile, and he returned it with one of his own, along with a pleasant tip of his head. He went back to his friends, I went back to my drink, and not long after, I left.

I was barely out of the door when someone's hand closed around mine, and I looked up in time to see Rashad rounding in front of me. "Hey," he said, his brow furrowed as he gazed down at me. "You're not leaving because of me, are you? If so, I'm—"

"No, no, not at all." I slipped my hand from his, closing it around my clutch purse. "It's time for me to head home anyway. Big day tomorrow."

His expression softened, but still held an edge of disbelief as he pushed his hands into the pockets of his jeans. "You sure? Cause—"

"Positive," I insisted, waving my hand toward the street to hail a passing cab.

The car stopped, and before I could get in good, Rashad was hanging in the passenger side window, handing several bills to the driver. "Take her wherever she needs to go, man."

"What the hell? Wait a minute, I don't need you to—"

"Accept it as my apology, please. For interrupting your night."

My face couldn't decide if it wanted to smile or scowl, so I settled for giving him a little nod as he stepped away from the car. "Thank you. Apology accepted."

He shot me another smile, then yelled, "Have a good night!" as the cab pulled away from the curb. Settling back against the leather seat, I finally allowed my mouth to spread into the smile it'd been threatening all night, then took a deep breath.

It wasn't *impossible*, not by a long shot, but unlikely that I would ever even see that man again, but still... I was almost embarrassed at the way my heart was still racing, palm still tingling from his touch.

Almost embarrassed.

Homeboy was *fine*.

With my head resting on the back of the seat, I maneuvered my phone out of my purse to check my correspondences. Inside my email app, I went down the line, checking off messages to sort into folders where I could answer in order of importance… some other time.

When I was done with my business email, I switched to my personal account, which somehow always still ended up full of spam and other non-personal things I never planned to read. There were a couple from my little sister Lauren, sending me links to fashion stuff. A few from my dad, articles he found interesting about military affairs and the like, and wanted to share.

And then… there was one from Drew, sitting there in my inbox like it was innocent and not full of lies, bullshit, and a happiness-seeking missile with the sole purpose of ruining the rest of my night. I stared at his name for the longest time before I finally tapped to open the message, holding my breath while I waited for it load.

"It's been a minute, B. I heard you moved… hit me up. Let's catch up. – Drew."

So many questions ran through my head. Catch up on what, exactly? Would he be leaving someone's bed to meet me? Lie to *her* face like he'd lied to mine? And why was he talking about it *being a minute* as if that shit was an accident? I hadn't seen him because I didn't *want* to see him…

Okay so maybe that wasn't completely accurate. I'd *seen* Drew, because he made himself seen. Although as a photographer, his job was technically *behind* the camera, he always seemed to make his way in front of it with one pretty young starlet or another, living it up and integrating himself into that lifestyle. And he'd *seen* me, because just like I couldn't resist googling him every once in a while to check on him, I had no doubt he'd been all over my blog, checking on me.

But screw him.

Anyway.

I took a deep breath, then hit the little trash can icon in the corner of my screen, tapped *yes* to confirm deletion, then went into my *trash* folder to permanently delete. No backsies. Never, *ever* any backsies.

I had notifications from nearly every social media app on my phone, so I tapped on the icon that would lead me to Facebook, not realizing that I'd tapped to open a specific message.

Shit shit shit shit shit.

As soon as I saw Drew's name on the screen, I hit the button to back out, but I knew it was too late. I'd opened the message, no matter how fast I closed it, and snitching-ass Facebook was going to *show* him not only that I'd seen it, but exactly what time as well.

Shit.

I glanced out the window at the traffic moving past,

then with a heavy sigh, I shook my head and turned my attention back to the phone. Against my better judgment, I opened the app again, taking a deep breath before I turned my eyes on the screen.

"B, where you at baby girl? You can't still be ignoring me."

Before I'd even finished reading that, another message popped up on the screen.

"And I know you're seeing my messages, it says it right here on the screen. So what's up? We just up and stop talking to people now?"

Ugh.

Not giving myself a chance to decide otherwise, I went to his profile page and unfriended him, trying to remember when I'd accepted him as a friend on a different account. I'd blocked him from communicating with me in this way a *long* time ago, back when we broke up. But… this was Drew. There was really no telling what kind of sneakiness he had going on. I then blocked him on *this* account too.

No. Backsies.

»——«

"Love is bullshit.

Wait.

Let me rephrase that, cause that's not exactly what I mean.

I don't have anything against love, okay?

I *love* my dad, I *love* my sister and niece, I *love* hibachi fried rice, I *love* my new place, I *love* my career, and being my own boss.

I *love* myself — being *me* is friggin' awesome.

I know *love*. I love *love*. I just think we'd all be better off without it.

Or maybe just me.

Maybe *I'm* better off without it.

Cause if I'm being real, like *for real for real*, romantic love has never brought me anything but stress and heartache, and damn near an arrest record, and *who needs that shit*? Who needs the constant questioning, the contrived selflessness, bending over backwards to keep your mate happy, and hoping they keep doing the same for you. Wondering, wishing, hoping that your love is enough to keep them from going astray. Hoping that *you're* enough to satisfy *their* needs.

And then when it ends, with the soul-crushing realization that whatever they were looking for, *you* weren't enough... what then? When you have to pick up the broken pieces of your life, figure out how to live without that person, what the hell do you do then? When you have to endure the sympathy from friends, ridicule from frenemies, *what then?*"

I held down my shift key and typed that question mark with enough of a *bang* that my whole desk shook, and my treasured last can of blood-orange San Pellegrino tipped over, spreading fizzy orange liquid across my desk.

Shit.

I snatched up my laptop, frowning as a stream of liquid dripped from the side. Biting the inside of my cheek to keep from cursing out loud, I placed the computer well out of reach of the puddle, grabbed a towel from the bathroom, and sat down to clean up my mess.

Just… chill Bianca. Tomorrow will be fine.

I probably should have been in bed anyway, but after showering, the last remnants of my drink at Urban Grind had worn off, leaving me wide-awake and unable to relax. *That's* what drove me in front of my computer to make an attempt to draft another blog post.

When I was done cleaning up my spilled drink, I pulled the laptop in front of me again, my eyes roving over the screen as I reviewed my words. By the time I reached that harshly-typed question mark, I'd come to a conclusion. Several, actually, with the first being that I would never, *ever* hit publish on *that*.

I highlighted the passage and hit the *backspace* key, then saved the newly empty draft, then completely deleted the post, then purged it from my *trash* bin for good measure. No backsies. That bitter post wasn't the only thing I purged, either. Along with it went the idea that I should post about relationships on my blog or YouTube channel *anyway*.

Lavish on the Low was a fashion and beauty blog, geared toward women who wanted to look great on a tight budget. I delivered a new post every other day, and a bi-weekly vlog to boot. But still, when I dove into the comments, there were always people — usually young girls — asking for more. They wanted to see the *real* Bianca. They wanted me to talk about self-esteem, body issues, health, and spirituality. I got emails all the time, asking me for advice about what to do about a boyfriend who did this, or that.

Aside from the fact that *me* giving advice about keeping a relationship together was hysterically funny, I simply didn't want to do it. It felt too personal, like way too much information, but then I kept seeing articles that said maybe I *should*. People didn't *only* want to see me model or talk about cute clothes and makeup, they wanted insight into my *life*. Something to give them a glimpse of who I really was, and how I interacted with the people who *really* knew me.

I could talk about confidence. I could show them a few yoga poses. But showcasing my jaded feelings about love and relationships to two hundred thousand subscribers?

No. Friggin. Thanks.

I flipped my laptop closed and headed for my closet, tossing the orange soaked towel into the laundry basket as I passed. Midnight had come and gone, so the meeting at Sugar&Spice magazine was technically today — in less than twelve hours, actually. I still hadn't chosen anything to wear, which was unlike me. In order to successfully run my blog, I kinda *had* to be organized, and strategic about what I wore in public. But this was *different*. What criteria was I supposed to use when deciding what to wear to meet a woman like Cameron Taylor, who was basically my idol?

She was only in her thirties, but had built an online magazine that rivaled the *giants* in the industry in website views and ad revenue. Sugar & Spice got exclusive celebrity interviews, permission from the parents themselves to debut celeb baby pictures, etc. Some savvy paparazzo had even snapped a picture of the first lady reading S&S from her smartphone.

Cameron Taylor was a big damned deal.

Sugar & Spice was a big damned deal.

This *meeting* was a big damned deal.

Part of the magic of Sugar & Spice was that it was still a pretty small operation, by design. In an interview, Cameron said she kept it that way to preserve the integrity of what she put out. Besides the celebrity stuff, she was still big on supporting local small business, and putting out credible news stories that *mattered*. She wanted the magazine to have broad appeal, while still being accessible, which is where I came in.

I was a faithful reader of S&S, so when I saw they were looking for bloggers to partner with for columns in different interest categories... I went for it. I was completely unmoved by not being the "biggest" in my niche, because I believed I was one of the *best*. I may not have had the most subscribers, or biggest sponsorships for my blog, but I worked hard, and I put out quality content. So... I entered.

Imagine my surprise when they actually *called*.

So, the hardest part was over. They liked my entry video enough to want to meet in person, and the success of the blog spoke for itself. I'd *earned* this meeting by simply being myself, letting my personality shine through in my vlogs and through my wardrobe. There was no need to make it all... difficult.

I flipped off the light in my closet and climbed into my bed, turning on the TV. Old episodes of *Girlfriends* played in the background while my mind drifted to Urban Grind. There was a time, *before Drew*, when I would have flirted my little heart out with a man like Rashad. Tall, handsome, charming… exactly the right recipe for a few months of fun.

Maybe I should have been nicer.

But it didn't matter now.

What mattered was getting to sleep so I could be fresh for this meeting.

two

. . .

bianca

MY HEART WOULDN'T STOP RACING.

I smoothed my hand over my white blazer one more time, praying that they were clean as I stood in the bright, sunlit conference room at the Sugar&Spice offices. There were about ten other people in the room, all waiting for apparently the same thing as me. I glanced around, wondering which one— or *ones* of these other bloggers were my competition.

"Fill out a sticker and slap it on!"

I turned in time for a petite woman with creamy brown skin and thick, gorgeous hair cut into a chin-length bob to push a miniature clipboard into my hands. There was a marker attached to the top, and a large name tag secured to the board's flat surface.

"You should put your first and last name — or whatever go by — along with your blog name, and niche. Please people, *try* to write legibly." Denise, executive assistant, Sugar&Spice, according to *her* nametag, beamed at us, then headed back to the front of the room.

In neat script, I wrote *Bianca Bailey – Lavish on the Low – Fashion/Beauty*, on my name tag, then tucked the clipboard under my arm to pull the protective backing off. I stuck it to my blazer, hoping like hell I wouldn't have a problem removing it later, then stacked my clipboard on the table with the others.

With that done, I resumed my sweep of the room, looking for my opposition. My eyes landed on a tall & sexy with golden skin, thick sandy hair, cut into a low fade on the sides, and gray-green eyes, standing with the only other male bloggers there. He was dressed well — nice jeans, nice sweater, with green undertones that complimented his eyes. My gaze slid over to his name tag, and I eased a little closer under the guise of looking out of the large picture window to read it.

Kieran Duke – First And Goal – Sports.

Okay... so he wasn't in my niche. I turned my eyes back to his face for a second look, only to realize he was doing the same thing. The corner of his mouth turned up in a little smirk, and he tipped his chin in greeting before I looked away. *That* was definitely not what I was there for.

A middle-eastern girl in fly, cognac-colored boots had caught my attention when the door from the lobby opened, and another blogger flounced in. Big, sexy curls, deep golden brown skin, thick lashes and eyes a shade darker than her skin... It didn't take long to recognize her as the gorgeous girl from last night, with the equally gorgeous brother.

She smiled as soon as she noticed me, and rushed over, pulling me into a hug. *"Oh, my, gosh, small world, huh?"* she giggled as she squeezed me tight, pushing her hair away from her forehead as she ended our forced embrace. She turned to face Denise as she approached, graciously accepting a clipboard to write down her name and information.

While she filled it out, I studied her. She wore a thick, creamy white sweater, black skinny jeans, and multicolor, python print So Kate's.

Ah, hell.

I held my breath while she finished her name tag, and she looked up at me with a smile as she held the paper in front of her. "Before long, I'll be hyphenating this name." She gave a contented little sigh, and my eyes fell to the substantial diamond engagement ring on her hand. She tossed the clipboard onto the table with the others, pulled the back from her sticker with a flourish, then slapped the tag onto the front of her sweater.

Raisa Martin – Gluesticks and Glitter — Craft/DIY.

My shoulders sagged in relief.

Hallelujah.

"Are you okay?" Raisa asked, draping her arm around my waist like we'd known each other forever.

"Yes, I'm fine. Just a little nervous." I weighed the benefit of maneuvering away from her. I'd just moved here, had no friends, and Raisa was obviously part of the blogging community. I couldn't afford to end up with a reputation as a bitch, and anyway... she smelled like sugar cookies.

The arm could stay, for now.

Raisa pulled her face into a frown. "For *what*? Girl, the hard part is behind us, it's time to celebrate!"

"Umm, not until we know who got the segments."

Her frown deepened, and then her expression softened into a sheepish smile. She gave the room a conspiratorial glance, then lowered her voice as she dropped her mouth to my ear. "*Ooops,*" she whispered. "I forgot I was going by *insider* information. Don't say anything to anyone, but this isn't an interview. This is a *welcome*. Everybody here got a segment."

I pulled away from her then, and it was *my* turn to frown. "That's not how they made it seem over the phone."

"So nobody would spill the beans ahead of time. They want to announce it first, on their site and social media. Why do you think we had to check our phones in at the desk?"

Hmm.

Now that she mentioned it, I was feeling a little naked without any of my devices, but I thought it was to protect their privacy, or for security reasons. *Not* that they were keeping any of us from scooping their big announcement.

"Anyway," Raisa said, flipping her hair over her shoulder. "About last night... girl I've *never* seen my brother run after anybody like that. I *hope* it was to apologize to you."

"Oh, um... yeah. He actually paid for my cab home."

Her eyes widened in surprise, not enough to be dramatic, but enough to notice, before she schooled her expression into nonchalance. "Oh... cool. *Good.* He's not a bad guy, but that mouth of his gets going, and you see what happens? I wonder how he's gonna react to seeing you here today..."

"Seeing me *here*?" For some reason, the thought of him brought heat to my cheeks, and a sudden, familiar tightness to my chest. "What... is he a blogger too?"

Raisa scoffed. "*Definitely* not. But... if you don't already know..." She shook her head, wagging a finger in the air for emphasis. "I've already spilled the beans on one thing... not gonna ruin *this* surprise."

»——«

Cameron Taylor was gorgeous.

I mean, I knew that from the pictures I'd seen of her at events, from photoshoots, all of that, but in person... she was insanely beautiful. Glowing mahogany skin, cheekbones to die for, and a jet black, perfectly styled pixie cut similar to mine. She didn't even have to announce herself when she walked into the room for my attention to turn to her. It gravitated to her presence.

"Good afternoon everyone," she said, smiling at all of us gathered around the conference room table. "I'm sure that by now each of you has noticed that you are the *only* blogger here representing your niche. From that, I'm *also* sure that you've concluded that the video segments, along with the columns on the website... are *yours*."

She paused for a moment, grinning as a collective buzz of excitement went around the table. "Now, I didn't choose you all based on popularity. I chose you based on what I could see of your work ethic, your reputation, and the obvious sweat equity you've put into your careers. *None* of you are the biggest in your niche, but my team and I believe that you either already *are* or could be, the *best*. There is no competition here. I want to see you all working together, elevating each other."

My heart caught in my chest as she looked directly at me and smiled. "I want to see Keiran directing his subscribers who have partners or friends with no interest in sports analysis over to Bianca's fashion vlogs. Bianca should be directing her readers to Raisa's DIY tutorials to hack their closets for better storage. Raisa's readers will be hungry after all that DIY — let's send them to Asha for some great recipe videos. This keeps everybody relevant, keeps everybody engaged. Keeps everybody *happy*. Talk to each other, collaborate, share ideas. There's room for everybody, but these segments are only on a trial basis. If you're not getting views, not pulling numbers... I will not keep you. *Community* is the name of the game around here for these next few months, okay?"

I nodded along with everyone else, but she could have

told us we had to do a gladiator style death match, complete with coliseum, and I would have readily agreed.

She was Cameron friggin' Taylor.

"Alright, so I'm considering today sort of a meet and greet," Cameron continued, straightening her chic denim blazer. "We've got a late lunch from Honeybee set up for you in the banquet area, and I want you all to meet, and mingle. Some of you already live within an hour or two of the city, but you may not know each other, and some of you traveled to be here today, and plan to do this thing from a distance. This may be the only time you're all together in person until the anniversary event, which is about six weeks from now. Get to know everybody, make friends. We'll be pulling you individually for one on one meetings, and to have your photos taken for the press release and film your bios on the S&S website."

Photos taken?!

I immediately, *silently* panicked, kicking myself for my outfit choice that morning. I'd played it safe, in my white blazer, grey skinny jeans, nude top and nude booties. Cute, but *definitely* not fashion-idol material.

Digging my nails into my palms, I blinked tears away from my eyes. I would *not* cry over a bad outfit choice, especially not in front of a room full of people. Not even when wearing the right thing was my *job*, and I'd already dropped the ball. Nope. I *would not do it.*

Along with everyone else, I stood and followed another assistant from the conference room, into an area that was obviously decked out for a party. The food smelled *heavenly,* and I was starving after skipping lunch because I was too nervous to eat, but I couldn't make myself touch anything.

I was *still* too damned nervous to eat.

I wasn't really in a mingling mood, so I headed to the far end of the room, away from the food, but Raisa grabbed me by the hand, squealing as she pulled me away from everyone else.

"Ohmigosh, isn't it *exciting,*" she gushed, squeezing my fingers between hers. "Filming bios, pictures for press releases, it feels so…big!"

Big was an understatement. It felt *huge,* and I felt *hugely* unprepared. How much time would I get for the bio, what should I say? What should I *do*? There was no doubt in my mind that this was planned with a purpose, to see how we handled pressure, but *still.* This was nuts.

"Excuse me ladies…"

I looked up from my internal freak out to see the Kieran standing over Raisa and me. He was even sexier up close, and he had his eyes fixed on *me* — probably because of that big-assed rock on Raisa's finger.

"I just wanted to introduce myself," he said, his voice carrying the barest hint of an accent as he shook first Raisa's hand, then mine. "Kieran Duke, First and Goal." He kept my hand tucked in his longer than he needed to, and finally I pulled away, glancing at Raisa in time to see her attempting to hide a smirk.

"Bianca Bailey, Lavish on the Low. Raisa Martin, Gluesticks and Glitter." I pointed at myself, then Raisa, hoping it would communicate that we were done, but he didn't budge.

"Raisa Martin... any relation to Rashad Martin?" Kieran finally turned his attention away from me, and I started to sneak away but Raisa looped her arm through mine, keeping me close.

She nodded. "Rashad is my brother, but no nepotism here." She pressed a hand to her chest like she was giving her word, ending her declaration with a big grin.

My mouth was already open to ask how *he* knew Rashad when Raisa glanced back, and must have quickly deduced what I was about to do, because the next thing I knew, she was resting a hand on Kieran's arm. "You know, Bianca was telling me she doesn't understand the bracketing system for the college basketball championships. Can you explain that to her please while I go grab a snack?"

Before I could object, Raisa was gone, and Kieran was starting up an explanation on the process of elimination in championships, complete with a breakdown of different conferences.

I shook my head, holding up a hand to stop him. "Kieran, please. I am so sorry, but you're like... speaking German to me right now. I have no idea what you're talking about."

Pushing his hands into his pockets, he lifted an eyebrow. "But I thought Raisa said—"

"Raisa was causing a distraction. I understand the basics of sports, and that's all I care to understand."

"Ah, so you're one of *those* girls."

I narrowed my eyes, even though my mouth wanted to break into a smile. *"Those* girls?"

He gave a quiet chuckle, then ran his thumb over his bottom lip. "Yeah. Ones who'd rather chop a bucket full of onions than watch a basketball game."

"Are you implying that a woman's place is in the kitchen while you watch that game?" I asked, propping a hand on my hip as my face descended into a scowl.

Immediately, his sexy little smirk dropped, and his eyes widened. "What? *No,* I meant an undesirable task... unless you *like* chopping onions, then by all means chop away. I'm down with the feminist cause, do your thing."

At those words, I let a bit of softness creep onto my face, and lowered my shoulders from my defensive stance. "Mmhmm. For what it's worth... I *hate* onions, but I would *still* rather chop them than watch basketball."

Kieran stepped back as a big grin crossed his face. He had a gorgeous smile, and I had to consciously pull my gaze away before it lingered into a stare, and bite my bottom lip to keep from breaking into a big grin of my own.

"So you're giving me a hard time for nothing then, huh?"

I shrugged, keeping my gaze cast somewhere to the left of him, but not so far that he wasn't still in my view. "Basically."

He shook his head as he laughed. "I can appreciate your honesty, Bianca. I may as well be honest too." He leaned forward, lowering his mouth to my ear, and the minty coolness of his breath tickled my face as he quietly spoke, "I don't know shit about fashion."

He pulled away then, giving a similar shrug to mine as he looked around, pretending to be afraid someone was listening in. "I'm man enough to admit that my *grandmother* dressed me this morning, via Skype."

"Stop playing."

"I'm *not*," he insisted, lifting his hands. His brow dipped into a serious expression as he hunched over a little. "*Wear somethin' green, baby. Bring out ya' eyes.*" Somehow, Kieran kept a straight face as he mimicked his grandmother in a high-pitched, wavering tone, but I broke into a giggle that I swiftly quieted with a hand over my mouth.

"Oh my goodness," I mumbled through my fingers. "You need to quit."

"I'm *serious*, girl," he chuckled. "That's what she said, and this was the only thing green I had in the closet. And I think *she* sent it to me. So... yeah, I don't know anything about any of that stuff, but... I do know you're gorgeous."

Oh.

That was... unexpected. Heat rushed to my cheeks as Kieran's gaze swept over me. He pulled his bottom lip between his teeth as our eyes met again, and I swallowed hard, willing myself to keep my voice even as I replied.

"Um... thank you," I said, knowing even as I spoke that my response was wack. But... flirting wasn't my thing, not really anymore, and he'd caught me off guard.

I may have been out of practice, but Kieran picked up my slack, giving me a broad smile. "You are *very* welcome, but I'm just telling the truth. The hair, and the piercings… it works for you. But I mean… you already knew that, right? You're the expert."

"I don't know about—"

"Kieran?"

I glanced around Kieran, and he turned to see Denise standing behind him, wearing an amused grin as she glanced between us. "Sorry to interrupt, but Mr. Duke, we're ready for your one on one, if you'll follow me."

"Well… I guess that's my cue," he said, giving me a little salute as Denise headed to the door. "It was nice meeting you, Bianca."

"Likewise." I turned away then, to avoid the temptation to watch him walk through the door. Less than a second later, Raisa was at my side, looping her arm through mine.

"So that looked *fun*," she said, wearing a big smile as she nudged me with her elbow.

Shaking my head, I made a quick attempt to get away, but she was stronger than she looked, and tugged me closer. "*Uh-uh.* Tell me what happened."

I groaned. "*Well,* after your little sneak attack, we talked a little, he made me laugh, then he left for his one on one. The end."

"Oh girl *please*," Raisa said, pursing her lips. "It looked like much more than that. It looked like *flirting* to me."

"Well I don't know what to tell you." I shrugged, then successfully extricated myself from her grasp. "Even if he *was* flirting, I'm not available, so… doesn't really matter does it?"

Raisa's eyes widened. "*Oh.* I'm sorry, I didn't even think to ask if you were involved with someone."

I swallowed hard, then managed a smile. "I'm not. Just... not available. Not for a relationship or anything like that, so... yeah."

For a short moment, Raisa studied me, seemingly unsure of what to do, but then her face brightened into a smile. "Well that doesn't mean we can't check out all the other cute boys and girls, now does it?"

Somehow, she got her arm looped through mine again, and this time I let it stay as she dragged me into the middle of the room with the other bloggers. My gut reaction was to be bothered by her instant enthusiasm for our sudden friendship, but it was overwhelmed by the fact that her bubbly personality made me feel a little less nervous. Not to mention that fact that she hadn't looked at me with pity, or pressed the issue when I said I was unavailable. She accepted it and moved on, which was refreshing as hell.

We mingled with the other bloggers, waiting as our names were called one by one. Kieran came back — as everyone did — after his one on one, but I didn't offer anything that he might take as encouragement to approach me again. The last thing I wanted to do was send the wrong message, that I was interested in him as anything other than a colleague. Yeah, he was cute, and yeah, he made me laugh, but... so did Drew at first.

Comparing the two wasn't fair, I know, but still. Kieran and Drew had a similar *you can trust me, cause look how sexy and adorable I am* kinda charm, and I wasn't really trying to go there again. Been there, and had "scorned" and "jaded" tee shirts in every damn color. I preferred to stay where I was, firmly rooted in the reality that romantic love was another gadget in the *master manipulator* toolkit.

But I was jumping the gun anyway. All Kieran had done was told me I was pretty.

Get a friggin' grip, Bianca.

"Ms. Bailey?"

My heart leapt up into my throat at the sound of Denise calling my name. It meant it was time for my one on one, and fear and exhilaration washed over me at the same time as I waved goodbye to Raisa and the others to follow Denise from the room.

"Don't be nervous." Denise shot me a smile, making me wonder how terrified I must have looked if she felt the need to offer comfort. We traveled through a small waiting area with a desk, and she opened the door into a larger room, ushering me inside.

There was a comfortable-looking arm chair — presumably for me — situated slightly away from a semi-circle of five others. Cameron sat in the last chair on that end, and Denise directed me to her first. She stood, and I extended a trembling hand in greeting, but she waved it away with a smile. "Girl I don't do that handshaking stuff, give me a hug!" My eyes bulged as she pulled me into a warm, familiar hug, and I was still a little dazed when she stepped back, putting a hand on my shoulder. "It is a pleasure to meet you, Bianca. Welcome to the Sugar&Spice."

I didn't have much chance to freak out, because the next thing I knew, we were skipping the empty seat to Cameron's immediate right, and I was shaking hands with Audrey Ames, one of Sugar&Spice's head writers. Natalie Patton, another head writer, was next, and on the other side of her... Rashad.

I pressed my lips together to keep my mouth from dropping open in surprise, but I knew he picked up immediately on who I was, because of the cool little smirk playing at the corners of his mouth.

What the hell is he doing here?

I knew the people that comprised Sugar&Spice's executive staff like the back of my hand, and it was the four women, Cameron, Denise, Audrey, and Natalie. *Not* Rashad. Even so, as I wracked my brain for how in the world he fit into this picture, something snapped into place. If Raisa's last name was Martin, and Rashad was her brother, that would make *him* Rashad Martin, whose name I'd seen in the photo credits on the S&S website about a million times.

Sure enough, Denise introduced him a moment later as Rashad Martin, adding on that just that morning, he'd been given the *official* title of head photographer and videographer for Sugar & Spice magazine. I swallowed hard, then extended my hand, but he gave it a look of disdain similar to Cameron's.

"I prefer hugs too," he said, stretching his arms toward me with a wink. His face spread into a bigger smile as he gave me a *come here* motion with his fingers, bringing forth a single dimple that I hadn't noticed the night before. I was a *sucker* for dimples — lucky for me he only had one.

"Rashad..." Cameron's voice carried a warning edge as it traveled from the other side of the semicircle.

Rashad groaned, then dropped his arms as he sucked his teeth, looking past me to his boss. "Man, when are you gonna stop being a hater, Cam?" I didn't know whether to laugh or be alarmed at his overly-familiar retort to *the* superior, but I was thankful when he put out his hand for what I *thought* would be a quick shake. Instead, he gently squeezed my hand in his, holding on longer than necessary, and damn if the electric tingle traveling between us didn't make me feel a little weak in the knees.

"Bianca Bailey," he said, in a distinctly sensual tone as his gaze traveled from my name tag up to my face. "Pleasure to meet you."

I gave him a little nod, then pulled my hand away, clasping them in my lap as I sat down. His attention was focused on me, but I refused to look his way. Cameron turned on the screen of her tablet, looked at me, and smiled.

"Alright, Bianca. Let's talk about your new relationship with Sugar & Spice magazine."

three

. . .

rashad

RIGHT AFTER COLLEGE, way, *way* past the time he sat me down to have *"the talk"*, my father warned me about women who were trouble. Nothing about *"fast-tailed girls"*, or anything like that, more like… an explanation of how to peep out the kinda trouble to avoid, and the kinda trouble you just… *couldn't.* According to my dad, my mother was that kinda trouble for him.

A woman who caught you off guard, and made your brain go a little bit haywire, who you couldn't keep off your mind no matter how hard you tried. And *that* was just the beginning. The way he explained it, once they were in your head, there was no way you could resist the magic between their legs, and once they'd given you the best mental and physical fuck of your life, they burrowed their way into your heart, and there was no way you were getting out of *that.*

Funny thing was, he explained it to me like it was something to *aspire* to. Nothing about the idea of getting stuck under one woman appealed to me. At twenty six... I was still young, still enjoying sampling different flavors.

My father loved the hell out of my mother though, so I guess I shouldn't have been surprised. Just last week, Raisa and I called ourselves popping in for a surprise visit to their suburban house, and ended up seeing *way* more of our naked ass, apparently *freaky* ass parents on the piano than we ever wanted to see.

But anyway, the point is, if I had to guess... Bianca Bailey was exactly the kinda trouble my dad was talking about. All week, she'd been on my mind. Even before I found out about her paid internship at the magazine, that's where she'd been, from the time she turned those big brown eyes on me and called me spoiled and arrogant. A pretty — like *forreal* pretty— woman with a smart-ass mouth was damn near irresistible to me.

She was a problem.

Luckily, we didn't really work together, so I hadn't even seen her all week. Well... I may have watched a couple of her YouTube videos, and... blew through a few hours skimming through every post on her blog from the last two years, but that didn't mean shit.

I was supposed to be staying away from *trouble*. And I was... kinda.

Raisa had invited me to her house for drinks and food, but I didn't realize the guest list would include a few of the bloggers. I was beyond glad to *not* see wack-ass Kieran, who'd spent the entire filming of his bio cracking corny sports jokes that women ate up because he had green eyes. I was trying *not* to be glad that I *did* see Bianca.

She was off in a quiet corner by herself, tapping away at the glowing screen of her smartphone, looking like *exactly* the kind of trouble I wanted to get into, if I was gonna get into it. After seeing her in action at the meet and greet, plus the filming of her bio, I could fully appreciate just how much her appearance contradicted who you might assume she was.

Rich, deep brown skin, big brown eyes, and a nose ring. Not the tiny silver ball, either. A septum piercing, right through her cute little nose, eye-catching and ornate, the type of thing that typically would have made me cringe, but... she was still so goddamned *pretty*. She wore her hair in a pixie cut that flattered that pretty-assed face. Mixed in with inky-black strands, chunks and wisps of her hair were bleached white-blonde, and tinted with lavender.

Purple hair, nose ring, tattoos, and a pierced eyebrow all should have said edgy, but... she was fucking... *pretty*.

She raised that neatly-arched eyebrow at something on her phone, and before I could wonder what she was reacting to, her eyes were on me. They were glossy, which meant whatever Raisa put in the punch had caught up with her too, and she was a little tipsy. But they were still bright, and she was alert, staring at me like she was trying to figure something out.

Maybe like why I was staring at her.

Shit.

I looked away, pretending to be into the conversation. Sinking back into the plush cushions of the arm chair I'd claimed when I came in, I chuckled along when everybody broke into laughter over something Gabe, Rai's fiancé said.

Unfortunately, same as that first night I saw Bianca, they were talking about relationships again. Or at least they *were*. It was starting to get late, so people were saying their goodbyes to leave. Soon, it was just me, my "twin" Raisa, — mama and daddy weren't really trying to hear that *wait six weeks before sex* nonsense, so we were barely a year apart in age — her fiancé, Gabe, and Bianca, who was still distracted. I glanced over at my sister, who winked, then cut her eyes to Bianca, like she just *knew* that was the kind of girl I liked.

Because, again... *pretty*.

Hell yeah I liked her.

But I was supposed to be off that.

No distractions, no *trouble*, only laser focus on my goals. My boss — even though I thought of Cam as more like another big sister than anything else — had threatened to repossess my promotion to head staff photographer at Sugar & Spice magazine if I didn't finish the final edits for next month's images before the weekend was over. I'd heard that threat enough times to know it was empty, but I still didn't want to let her down. So... instead of the *usual* kinda fun I would have on a Friday night... I was here with Raisa and Gabe... and Bianca.

"Yo, B!" Rai called out. Bianca looked up with her eyebrows raised, first at me, then Raisa. "C'mere. Put your phone down for two seconds and come talk to *us*. I didn't invite you over here to make the place look better, and now everybody is gone."

Bianca ran her tongue over her dark painted lips, then pushed off from the wall, slowly making her way into the seating area. When she got closer, she smiled — at Raisa, not me, then shoved her phone into the back pocket of her jeans. She pulled her thick, oversized sweater up from where it had slipped down, covering up a little glimpse of tattooed shoulder as she took the empty seat across from me. Not even five seconds later, she'd fished her phone out of her pocket again, and pressed the button to turn on her screen, but one glance at Raisa's expression made her turn it right back off.

"Sorry. Trying not to fall behind on my email."

Damn. Even her voice is pretty.

My eyes fell to the "LotL" logo printed on the back of her phone case, and my thought traveled to a video I'd seen on her channel, when she was *so* excited to show her subscribers that logo. Her hair was blonde back then, and she didn't have the septum ring, but that pretty-ass face was the same. That video was from two years ago, but she seemed so much *younger*, so much less... serious back then. She was bubbly, almost to the point of being goofy. The kind of girl you could kick it with.

Now, she seemed poised, and held a certain... pragmatism ... that told me she *definitely* wasn't my type. She was one of *those* chicks, the type that demanded to *know where they stood with you* and *where you saw the relationship going* before you could get more than the head in, and that was all I was really trying to do.

Because... *trouble.*

"Oh you know I get it," Raisa said. "Life of a blogger. But remember, we said we were putting work away for the night, *right?*"

Bianca groaned, then gave Rai a sheepish smile. "*I remember.*"

"Mmhmm. Alright then, your turn."

"My turn for what?"

Her eyes fell on me, like she thought I might have the answers, but I shrugged. I'd been watching *her* instead of the conversation.

"Your turn to confess the craziest thing you've ever done in a relationship."

For several long seconds, Bianca stared at Rai like she was waiting for her to deliver a punchline. When none came, she blew out a slow breath and sat back, shaking her head. "I... I think I'm gonna um...*pass,* on this particular line of questioning."

"*Noooope!* You don't get to *pass,*" Raisa said, patting Bianca on the shoulder as she passed her to get to the table full of shots. "You drink, and then you *answer.*"

She pushed a hot pink jello shot into Bianca's hand, then picked one up for herself. I halfway expected Bianca to refuse, but she grinned, raising the shot glass in a mock toast before lifting it to her mouth to knock it back.

When she was done, she shook her head, then glanced around the room. Her eyes landed on me again for a brief second, and then she flicked them away, looking up at the ceiling. She pushed out a heavy sigh, ran her tongue over her lips, and then said, "Okay... um... I went to my last boyfriend's house... with a gun."

There was a moment of silence as we all stared, wide eyed, wondering if she was serious. Or at least *I* was. Bianca smiled, but I could tell from the lack of warmth in her glossy eyes that it was forced. She chewed at her top lip like she was nervous, then cleared her throat as everyone calmed down.

"I *never* would have guessed something like that for you, B! Are you *serious*?" Raisa gushed. "Are you serious?"

Bianca shrugged. "Unfortunately... yes. We were together for a really long time, and were really, *really* close, but then... he changed. *We* changed. He did some things that were really foul, and I... I just snapped."

Raisa scooted forward, almost to the edge of her seat as she craned her head in Bianca's direction. "So, *what the hell happened*? Girl did you pistol whip him?!"

"Did I— *what*? *No*," Bianca contended, raising her palms in innocence as she laughed. "No, nothing like that. Nothing at all, actually." She ran her pink tongue over those plush, deep crimson lips again as her mood visibly sobered. "I got to his place, used my key to get in, and... he had a girl there. I could hear them in his bedroom going at it, and I asked myself what the hell I was doing. Why was I there, about to end up in jail, when I *knew* he and I should have been over? So... I went home, I drank a bottle of wine, and... I lived. We broke up. The end."

Raisa let out a low whistle. "Geez, Bianca! So what—"

"Uh-uh!" Bianca shook her head, then laughed. "The game was to confess your craziest thing, and that's it. I've already said *more* than enough. I don't wanna talk about him."

"But wait a minute," I said, clearing my throat. Call me crazy, but my interest was even further piqued now. Little Miss Poised and Polished took shots, and was willing to *pop* somebody.

Sexy as hell.

She turned to me, her smile fading into apprehension as she met my gaze. "Yeah?"

"What were you gonna do? Were you gonna *shoot* him?"

"*No,*" she responded, rapidly shaking her head. "I never planned to hurt him, just... scare him, I guess."

"Scare him into what?" I pressed, knowing I was stepping on shaky ground since she'd *just* said she didn't wanna talk about it anymore, but... I really wanted to know. I'd always been interested in knowing what made women snap and do this type of crazy shit. "I mean, you don't take a gun to somebody's house without some type of plan... what did you want?"

"*Rashad,* chill out." Raisa slapped my arm as Bianca tucked her phone into the little pouch connected to a strap on her wrist, along with her keys.

"Thanks for inviting me Rai," Bianca said as she stood. "I'm gonna go ahead and get home, it's late."

"Wait, my bad. I didn't mean to..." I let that apology trail away, as Bianca headed for the front of the apartment without even glancing my way, or acknowledging I'd said anything.

Shooting me a scowl, Raisa rose from her seat on the couch to intercept Bianca's path to the door. "Wait a sec, B. I mean... do you want me to give you a ride or something? Like you said, it's late, and you've been drinking."

Bianca shook her head, waving a hand to dismiss Raisa's concerns. "I'll be fine. I'll get a cab or something."

"Are you sure? Cause—"

"Yes, I'm sure."

Raisa turned to glower at me for a second, then back to Bianca. "I'm so sorry about him."

"Don't sweat it. I'll see you later."

The next moment, she was gone, and Raisa gave me a death glare as she stomped out of the living room. "Get your rude ass out!" she yelled from her bedroom, before she slammed the door.

Gabe, who'd had one too many and had been watching in silence, groaned as he dropped his head onto the back of the couch. "Damn, Shad. You know *I'm* the one that's gonna have to calm her down, right?"

"Sorry, future brother in law. I owe you a drink next time we're out," I said, stopping to shake his hand as I started my exit.

He sucked his teeth as he sat forward. "You owe me *three* drinks, bruh."

I chuckled, heading down the hall where Raisa had disappeared. "Whatever you say Gabe." I knocked on their bedroom door, two raps with my knuckle, three with my palm, then another with my knuckle.

"The hell do you want, Rashad, I said get out!"

I rolled my eyes at Raisa's yelled response. "I'm sorry I offended your friend," I said back, raising my voice so she could hear me through the door.

"Yeah, you should be! Bye!"

I shook my head. "Okay baby sis. I love you."

The door swung open enough for Raisa to peak her head out, delivering another glare. "I love you too... with your dumb ass." The door closed in my face, and I laughed as I turned away, leaving Raisa and Gabe's apartment.

I really *wasn't* trying to offend Bianca, I was just curious. Especially since she didn't "seem" like the type to fuck a dude up. Hell, even with the piercings and tats, she didn't *look* like the type to do it. So, by *my* estimation, either she was crazy as hell, or ole boy screwed her over pretty bad... or some combination. Either way, the shit was interesting. Why *wouldn't* I want to know?

Downstairs in the lobby, I spotted Bianca standing in the middle of the floor, staring down at her phone like before. She had her eyebrows pulled to the middle of her forehead as she paced, her fingers flying over her screen, tapping away. She gave it a harsh final tap — presumably hitting "send" — then dropped the hand holding the phone to the side as she used the other to wipe her face.

The sound of my footsteps drew her attention in my direction, and she cursed under her breath when she looked up. Shoving her phone into her back pocket, she headed for the door, but I jogged up, intercepting her.

"Hey, listen," I said, trying to get her to look me in my face. When she did, she crossed her arms, head tipped to the side in annoyance. I ignored that — and her watery eyes — to keep talking. "I didn't mean to cross a line, or whatever I did. I was being nosy, I didn't mean any harm. I'm sorry."

"Okay. Can you move, so I can leave?"

I raised my chin. "That's it? Just... okay, move?"

Her face wrinkled up like something smelled bad. "Uh... yeah? What did you expect?"

She shoved her way past me and out the door into the early fall air as I thought about that question. What *did* I expect?

The same thing you expect from other chicks, fool.

Hmm.

Maybe that was right. This certainly wasn't the first time I'd been checked for crossing a line, but typically an apology — a sincere one, because I really *hadn't* meant to upset her — and a smile was usually all it took to get makeup sex on the agenda. Now, it wasn't like that with me and Bianca, but she didn't even give me a smirk or anything. Hell, now that I think of it... she hadn't even actually accepted the apology, had only acknowledged that it existed.

Interesting. Really damned interesting.

It almost seemed like she wasn't really feeling me, but she was trying too hard for that to be true. Even though I knew damned well I should leave it alone… I pushed open the door and followed her outside.

"So what part of the city you headed to?" I asked, catching up with her on the sidewalk. "You wanna share a cab?"

She stopped her stride as I stepped in front of her, blocking her path. Speaking through her teeth, she replied, "None of your business… and no thanks. I *can* pay for my own transportation, you know?"

"I don't doubt that. Just… throwing out a suggestion."

She pressed her lips together in a line. "I see." Stepping around me, she continued her journey down the sidewalk, glancing up and down the street for an unoccupied cab.

"Bianca, come on," I said, catching up to her again.

She groaned, pressing a hand to her forehead before pushing it backwards through her hair. "*What?* What is it, Rashad, what do you want?"

"Damn, I'm just trying to talk to you. I think we got off on the wrong foot."

Frowning, Bianca shook her head a little. "And you think *tonight* was better?"

"I mean…," I blew out a gust of air through my lips, then pushed my hands into my pockets. "I guess not, and that's my bad. How about this — tell me what *would* be better."

I smiled at her after that, turning up the wattage enough to charm, but not so much that I looked like an idiot. To my surprise, her expression softened, and she stepped closer to me, tipping her head back to look into my face.

"You wanna make it better?" she asked, her voice softer… sexier.

"Yeah… what's up?"

She smiled then, lifting her hands to cup my face. "You can… leave me the hell alone. Thanks." She dropped her hands, then rolled her eyes, brushing past me as she continued down the street. A few seconds later, she flagged down a cab, and was gone before I could even move.

She played the hell outta me.

Guess she wasn't *playing* hard to get after all.

four

. . .

bianca

TO MAKE *him tell me he loved me.*

Not that I planned on ever telling him *that* part of the story, but that was the answer to Rashad's question. I went to Drew's house with an unloaded gun, to *force* him to give me the words he'd been withholding from me for months, because of some imaginary slight against him.

So damned stupid.

I couldn't even tell the lie that I was too overwhelmed with emotion to think straight. I *unloaded* the gun, because Drew had a slick mouth, and I was so angry that he just *may* have pissed me off enough to pull the trigger. I'd made light of it earlier, because it had been on my mind all day, because *he* had been on my mind all day. Because I'd *started* the day with bullshit from him.

It was… honestly a little baffling to me, that after everything, Drew couldn't leave me alone. But instead of doing right by me, showing me some real care and compassion *one* time in the nine-odd years I'd known him, he... woke me up with more emotional abuse. Because *now*, I recognized it for what it was.

"What's up, B? I see you're still tryna play mad, ignoring me, so Jess let me hit you up from her account. I heard about the gig with Sugar & Spice mag, is that why you moved? That's a good look. You'll be working with my homeboy, Rashad Martin. I'll tell him to keep an eye on you for me."

I read that, and rolled my eyes. First, I blocked *Jess*, because screw her. She was my old college roommate, who pretended to be my friend, who I found out was one of many "friends" of mine Drew was screwing. This was so, *so* like him, to send a seemingly innocuous message full of barely veiled disrespect. A year ago, something like this would have sent me into a tailspin, and that's what he wanted. Throw me off my game, so I could cry on his shoulder like I used to, so he could tell me more about how bad at everything I was, under the guise of a motivational speech. But not anymore. I *refused* to give him that power.

Because screw him.

And his *homeboy* Rashad.

Because if Rashad really was *homeboys* with Drew, that told me everything I needed to know about him, and as far as I was concerned, none of it was good.

Somehow, still, despite *everything,* I still liked to categorize our breakup as *oh, we both just changed, we grew into different people,* but that's not friggin' true. Drew is what he'd always been, my sixteen-year-old self was too much in love to see it. A manipulator, and a liar, and... not someone who deserved to be in my life. But I let him, and allowed him to groom me into the perfect little stupid girlfriend.

But I wasn't that anymore, *finally*. I was starting to *really* feel free now. I'd been to plenty of therapy, my blog — which Drew had discouraged — was thriving and growing, and I'd even had a few no-strings-attached flings. I could be... *Bianca*... whoever the hell she was.

Looking up at the mirror, I was surprised to see tears in my eyes. I quickly wiped them away, then finished removing my makeup and tending to my nightly skincare routine. Briefly, I wondered if I'd been a little too hard on Rashad. It wasn't fair to fault him for curiosity, especially not when *I* was the one who introduced the story. But still... he was friends with Drew — supposedly, because I wouldn't put it past Drew to lie — and that was enough reason to keep my distance.

He may not have done anything to me, but if *Drew* was the kind of company Rashad kept, any mistreatment I sent his way was doing another woman a favor.

»——«

I couldn't seem to get away from Rashad.

In fact, it seemed like the more I tried to avoid his mention, the more he was shoved in my face. None of it even came from Raisa, crazy enough. That was his sister —

and fast becoming my good friend — but she was intuitive enough to detect that I really didn't care for him, and acted accordingly.

The internet, however, was not so kind. I actually rarely saw Rashad, because I didn't technically work at Sugar&Spice, but ever since the announcement of the new segments, my subscribers certainly seemed to think I saw plenty of him. Our video bios had been replaced with somewhat generic written ones, accompanied by three photos from the day of the meet and greet. Only one was a posed shot, and the other two were candid, which surprised me, because I couldn't even remember seeing anyone with a camera.

The posed shot was really, really good, but the candids... those gave me chills. One of was of me standing near Cameron Taylor, who was outside of the frame, but I remembered the moment vividly. She was talking about goal setting to one of the other bloggers, but I was listening intently, eyes wide in awe, lips parted in an almost childlike sense of wonderment. That one picture captured so much of what I was feeling at that moment — the admiration, the absorption of wisdom, the overwhelming sense of *hell yes, this is the opportunity I needed.*

The other picture captured a moment I didn't remember as clearly. My lips were pursed, as if I were blowing out a cleansing breath, and my hands were at my side, fingers splayed. The body language said I was calming myself down — or at least, trying. My shoulders were tense, and my anxiety nearly oozed off the screen, but… my eyes were bright, excited… ready for the new adventure.

The photos were… amazing. And each of the photo credits said Rashad Martin.

I felt like I'd been in the twilight zone for not knowing what he looked like before now. But suddenly, I had girls swooning in blog and vlog comments over the fact that I'd worked with Rashad Martin. It was certainly no *flood*, but after 4-5 a day for a week, I was sick of hearing his name.

And then Cameron called me. Like… directly. On my cell phone.

I was on my way back from spending the weekend with my dad, sister, and niece. I tried to do that once a month, and maybe even more now that I live closer. With my move, my dad's house was the halfway point between my apartment and Lauren's college. I set up my *out of office* message responses, turned off my phone, and dug into that quality time with my family. My dad wanted coffee, cinnamon streusel muffins, quiet moments of prayer, reminiscence about my deceased mother, and fishing with his oldest daughter. And I gave it. My niece wanted piggyback rides and cuddles. Lauren wanted sushi, any clothes or jewelry I would send her way, and advice from her big sister about the charming boy at college who took her breath away but seemed like trouble. And… I gave it, while trying my best to keep my personal cynicism tucked away.

Two years ago, I'd dropped Drew for *good*, and ever since then, I'd been gaining back the things he'd robbed from me. The wonderful thing about these weekends was that dad and Lauren didn't only *take*. They gave as well. Patience, serenity, and dignity from dad. Happiness, and hope, and... a certain youthful energy from Lauren. By the time I was leaving my dad's home to board my flight back to the city, I was exhausted, but full.

It was evening when I stepped out of the airport terminal to catch a cab, and I turned on my phone to send quick texts to Lauren and my dad to let them know I'd landed safely. I ignored notifications that started popping up and stuck the phone in my pocket. I'd just left the only two people in the world who were important enough that it couldn't wait until I was back home.

In the cab, the phone started ringing, and I slid it out of my pocket far enough to see the screen. The caller ID told me that this was one of the numbers from a list all of the bloggers had been given, of potential contact numbers from Sugar&Spice.

At eight at night, on a Sunday?

Determining that it must be pretty important, I answered the call, holding the phone to my ear with my shoulder as I climbed out of the cab and paid the driver.

"Hello? Bianca? *Finally!*" Was the response to my greeting, in a voice I immediately recognized as Cameron's. I nearly dropped the phone in shock, but quickly recovered, dropping my bags to the lobby floor inside my building so I could have both hands free.

"Ms. Taylor?! Hi! I— I mean— how can I help you?

What do you need from me?" I stammered, swallowing hard as I waited for an answer.

"Well, my team has been trying to get in touch with you all weekend, with no luck. This was my last-ditch, emergency effort, and I'm very glad you decided to pick up. Are you healthy, is everything okay?"

Oh, crap.

"Yes, I'm fine. Was with my family and had everything disconnected. But, emergency? What's going on?"

Cameron chuckled. "Perhaps I shouldn't use such strong language, since I really do hate for other people to impose their last minute decisions as emergencies on me, but... that's exactly what I'm about to do to you Bianca, forgive me. I'm sure you noticed that none of the bios from the bloggers went up on the site with the announcement. That's because they were, quite frankly, boring as hell. It took me a couple of weeks to decide what I wanted to do, but Friday morning, I figured out that they needed to be re-shot, and... guided. Kind of like an interview. Do you get what I mean by that?"

"Yes ma'am."

"... ma'am?" Cameron's voice was full of disdain as she said that word, like it was a pejorative. "Please... call me Cameron."

Seriously?! My heart started racing at the thought of using such familiar language with her, but... if she *said* so, what else could I do? "Yes. I understand what you mean... Cameron."

"Good," she perked, the warmth coming back into her

voice. "In any case, I really wanted to get these shot over the weekend, so that Monday and Tuesday could be used for editing, and we could get these up on the site by Wednesday, with the weekly round of fresh articles. This would introduce you all, so that when it's time for your first real segments to air, the viewers already have a little taste of who you are, your personality."

"That sounds awesome."

"I'm glad you agree... cause I need you to do this *tonight.*"

My heart sank.

Shit.

I'd just stepped off a plane, I needed a shower, my hair hadn't been washed, I had no idea what to wear, I—

"You're the only one who hasn't filmed again yet," Cameron said, in response to my silence. "Like I said, I know it's last minute, but we really need this. And we can be flexible. The Sugar&Spice office is closed, but I can send him to your place, or he actually has a studio space set up in his—"

I groaned, running a hand through my frizzy hair. "Well, my place is a mess right now, so that's out. I guess I'm going to— wait a minute... He? He *who*?"

"Rashad. *But,*" she said, as if she already — rightfully — expected objection, "You can call a friend to go with you or something. Not that I think you're not *safe* around Rashad, because you absolutely are, but... I get the sense that the two of you may need a buffer between you. Maybe see if Raisa is available, she seems to bring out his best behavior."

Closing my eyes, I pinched the bridge of my nose between my fingers, avoiding the urge to groan again. "I... okay," I said, covered the phone's speaker with my hand so she wouldn't hear the heavy sigh I let out afterwards.

"Bianca, *thank you*. This really shows me how dedicated you are." She sounded so relieved that it *almost* killed my annoyance over having to work with Rashad.

Almost.

"It's not a problem, Cameron."

"Okay. Well... try to have fun with it, okay? Shad isn't a bad kid, but you have to remember not to take him too seriously."

Hmph.

"I'll keep that in mind, thank you."

After brief goodbyes, we hung up, and I dragged myself and my overnight bag to my apartment. Just outside my door, my phone chimed with details to contact Rashad, and I pressed my forehead to the heavy wood. I was already exhausted, and now I had to deal with *this* fool.

It was probably best to get coordinated sooner than later, so inside my apartment, I sent him a quick text.

"This is Bianca Bailey. Heard from Cameron. Where and what time can we meet tonight to film this bio? My place isn't an option."

Simple, and to the point. Satisfied with that message, I put my phone on the charger beside my bed, then took a quick shower and washed my hair. It naturally coiled into fat curls, so I dried it enough with a diffuser to leave the house without getting myself sick. Since it was for video, I kept my makeup light and neutral.

I was in the closet in my underwear, trying to pick out something to wear when Rashad's response came.

"I'm in for the night. Roll through whenever."

Roll through whenever? Ugh!

I rolled my eyes as I read his message again. *Roll through whenever* as if we were setting up a damned booty call!

"Can you send your address?"

Keeping it simple, I pulled down a sheer white button up, teal skinny jeans, grey leather riding boots, and a grey leather jacket completed me except for accessories. I was digging around in my jewelry collection when my phone chimed again.

"Of course, sexy. It's..." I shook my head at the first part of the message as I plugged the address into my phone. His building was in walking distance, just around the corner, and I was still deciding if that was a good thing or not when the phone chimed again. **"I'll be waiting for you."**

I lifted an eyebrow, then frowned at the phone as I tapped out a reply. *"Umm... do you know who you're texting?"*

"Of course. Pretty ass Bianca Bailey, from Lavish on the Low. Why do you ask?"

"You don't think you're being a little inappropriate?"

"Only a little? I need to try harder. ;-)"

Oh dear God.

I groaned, then thought about Cameron's advice to invite Raisa. But... I was a grown woman. Surely I could handle Rashad without interrupting big sister's Sunday night, especially this late.

It was a little after nine-thirty when I knocked on Rashad's door, fidgeting with the zipper on my jacket. I took a deep breath as I waited on him to answer, wondering how this thing was gonna go. Cameron had mentioned interview style... did that mean *Rashad* was going to be asking the... of *course* it did. We sure hadn't coordinated a time with anyone else.

Wonderful.

I was raising my hand to knock again when his door swung open. Now... I may not have particularly *liked* Rashad, but it was silly to deny that the man was attractive. Tall, handsome, charming, gorgeous brown skin... there wasn't anything to complain about. But... *shirtless* Rashad, with biceps and abs and obliques on display, was just... *sex*. And I was reasonably sure he *knew* it.

I closed my mouth and cleared my throat, lifting my eyes to his face. Sure enough, his lips were pulled into a smirk, and that damned single dimple was right there, begging me to touch it.

"Are you gonna keep me standing outside all night?" I asked, looking anywhere but at him. "I'd like to get this done so I can be home before midnight. And can you put a shirt on or something? Why are you half-naked?"

"You gonna turn into a pumpkin or something?" He stepped back, motioning for me to come in, and I stepped past him into an apartment that defied the conditions I *thought* he would live in. I expected borderline filth, but his place was clean. *Really* clean, not just the type where you could tell the host had shoved the mess in the closet. It was masculine, decorated in deep wood tones, greys, and sage-y greens. Enough to tell he lived alone, but well-designed enough that I could tell a woman's touch, probably Raisa's, had been all over.

"Where you gotta be at midnight, Cinderella?" he continued, coming up right behind me. "And I'm in my own apartment, I'm half-naked because I *feel* like it. I'm accommodating *you*, remember? Where've you been all weekend that nobody could get in touch with you?"

Instead of responding, I pressed my lips into a hard, annoyed line. He shook his head, chuckling as he turned away, showing me a back view that was nearly as delicious as the front. I followed him around a corner into another area — the studio set up Cameron had mentioned. It was messier here, in the way that small spaces usually are when you're trying to keep things confined to one place.

It was nice though. One wall draped all in white, the other exposed red brick. The window was in the bricked wall, but the drapes were closed since it was dark outside. There was a chair there, and an end table and lamp, and nice art on the walls. I was about to compliment him when Rashad tipped his head toward the chair, then said "I'll take you right here," with a wicked little grin on his face, and a wink.

I rolled my eyes at him, then moved toward the chair

and took off my jacket, draping it over the back before I sat down.

"You need anything before we get started?" he asked, fitting a camera onto the tripod across from me. "Some water, anything?"

"No thank you."

Rashad looked up from the camera, his face pulled into a scowl. "Come on, B. It's late, we're at my apartment, nobody else around. You can kill the formality."

I lifted an eyebrow. "What?"

"No thank you," he said, in a snooty accent, raising his chin for a moment before he laughed. "Come on, girl. It's *nah, I'm good.* Lighten up!"

I couldn't help laughing at how serious he seemed, but I knew he was right. If I didn't do my part, the video would look stiff and formal, which was exactly what Cameron *didn't* want. And *that* was what mattered. Not him pissing me off the week before at Raisa's, not what he might go back and tell Drew. *Only* that I got this done because it was important for my career.

Wiggling my shoulders, I shook the tension from my body and relaxed some into the chair as I waited for us to start. Inevitably, my eyes drifted back to Rashad, and that gorgeous body of his. This time, they traveled lower, to the front of his sweatpants.

Stop it, Bianca.

I looked away, focusing instead on his fingers as they moved skillfully over the camera, changing a setting here, refocusing something, then making an adjustment there. A couple of moments later, he asked if I was ready, and I nodded.

"Alright," he said, hitting a button I assumed to be *record*. "First up, why don't you tell the people who you are?"

"My name is Bianca Bailey, and I am the creator and girl-in-charge on my YouTube channel and blog, Lavish on the Low."

Glancing around the camera, Rashad smiled. "Okay. Tell us about it."

"Um, Lavish on the Low is content created with the intention of showing my audience how they can look really great, even if they may be on a limited budget. I do makeup looks with things you can find at your local drugstore or dollar store. I show natural skin care, made with things you probably already have in your fridge or pantry. I give instructions on thrifting with discerning eyes, so you don't waste your money, and mending your own clothes to *save* money. Proper laundry care, a little bit of hair care... things like that."

I ran my tongue over my lips, hoping I didn't ruin my lipstick and wishing I'd accepted his offer of water. It was a little hot under the lights, and now that I was actually answering the questions... I was a little bit nervous, even though it was just me and him.

"Sounds very interesting," he said, giving me a thumbs up. "Now... tell me why any of this matters."

I froze for a moment, trying to wrap my head around his question. "Excuse me?"

Rashad looked at me from the around the camera. "Tell me why what you do matters. What's important about it? What's your impact?"

What kind of question...

I swallowed hard, lowering my eyes as I searched my head for answer. Because... why *did* it matter?

"I...um...," I blew out a little sigh, then lifted my eyes to the camera again. "What I do matters, because... these women matter. The girls too, they matter. And... I think that really often, even if everything around you is going to shit, if you *look* good, it can make you feel better. Retail therapy can be awesome, but everybody — *most people* — can't afford to blow money at the mall every time they feel a little bit down. But what if you know that fifteen really well spent dollars can put you in an outfit that's on-trend, and makes you feel like you can take on the world? Or if you know that for less than four dollars, I can show you a lipstick that makes you feel like the sexiest thing on the planet? Or that the acne you've been battling for years can possibly be a memory if you introduce your skin to coconut oil. What I do is important because... I'd like to think I'm adding value to the lives of my readers and subscribers by offering tips and advice on *truly* affordable things they can do and buy to look better, which is absolutely related to feeling better."

I pressed my lips closed before I rambled on that question any further, and waited on Rashad to ask the next.

He kept his face behind the camera as he spoke. "You

don't think that's shallow? Focusing on appearance as a source of confidence?"

My nostrils flared a little, but I remembered that he was filming this. "Shallow or not... it's *fact* that people want to look good. It's also *fact* that when you look good, you tend to *feel* good about yourself, in general. First dates, first day of school, your cheating spouse's funeral, job interview, reception dinner, baby shower, and *every day in between*. Feeling good about your appearance gives you the energy to take on what can *often* be a really cruel world."

"Good answer. You mentioned first dates, so I feel like it makes the next question fair game. Are you looking for love, and where can our viewers apply?" He tipped his head to the side and winked at me.

I didn't *want* to smile, and encourage his nonsense, but I couldn't help it. Shaking my head, I chuckled a little before I looked straight into the camera lens. "Next question."

"Ah, come on. You're gonna leave us hanging like that?"

"I sure am."

"*Please*? You can't even tell *me* where to turn in my application?"

Biting my lip to suppress a smile, I glanced down at my hands before turning back to the camera. "There are no open positions. *Especially* not for you, Rashad. And I hope you're gonna edit this out."

After that, he peeked out and gave me another smile. "Okay, Okay. Now... it seems like at the end of your videos, you end on a motivational message. Tell us about that."

"Yes, I do. I know that people aren't tuning in, or

coming to my blogs to hear me preach, but the message of personal value is important enough to me that I share it anyway. For a good part of my life... much longer than I should have... I allowed someone to mistreat me, and strip me of my value." I stopped, clearing my throat before I continued. "I gave him room to make me feel that I couldn't do better than him, that I didn't *deserve* better than his bull... *nonsense*, and that wasn't true. It wasn't worth it, to him, to treat me well, and not just make me *feel* loved, but to *actually* love me. But that lack of worth to *him*, doesn't make it a universal truth. Not for me, and not for anyone else. Your self-worth is innate, not based on what you look like, or wear, or think, or do. It's part of you. You have it because you're human, you matter because you have a heart, you're worth everything, because there's breath in your lungs, and blood in your veins. Never, *ever* let anybody tell you different, and if they try, get the hell away."

Rashad watched me, intently, as I delivered that message, ending with much more passion than I intended. I was on the edge of my seat, and had to scoot back, taking a deep breath as he finally looked away from me, and his face disappeared again behind the camera.

"Is there anything else you want to tell people about your brand, Bianca?"

I shook my head, suddenly feeling incredibly drained. "No. I think that's all."

There was a short pause before he answered. "Okay. Well, I think you've done an incredible job showing our viewers the passion and purpose behind what you do, as well as the practicality. Thank you for speaking with us, and we look forward to our next segment with you, where we'll get a chance to see you in action."

"Thank you for the opportunity." I smiled then, hoping it reached my eyes, and gave a good visual for the end of the clip.

Rashad held up his pointer finger. "One more question," he said, stepping from behind the tripod. "Off the record." He pressed something on the camera and the lens retracted and closed, then he stepped over the cords and things on the floor to get closer to me. "The guy you mentioned in the segment… is that the one you pulled the gun on?"

Taking a deep breath, I nodded, then looked away, not really wanting to see any pity in his eyes. He made a sound, somewhere between a grunt and sucking his teeth, then said, "Damn. Should have shot his ass."

When my eyes returned to his face, he was smiling, and I gave him a weak one back as I stood and put on my jacket, then began making my way to the front door.

"Whoa, where you going?" he asked, getting in front of me as I tried to pass him. "Why are you always running from me?"

I frowned. "Running?"

"Yeah, running." He stepped a little closer… *too* close. "Seems like every time I say something you don't like, you're ready to go home. That night at UG, the night at Raisa's, *now*. What is it… you can't take a little heat?"

Crossing my arms over my chest, I met his gaze. "I can take plenty of heat, thanks. Nobody is running from your ass, I'm done talking. We've accomplished what I came over here to do, so I'm going home. It's as simple as that."

"Is it?"

"*Yes*," I snapped, as my frown deepened into a scowl. "Rashad, nobody is thinking about your ass hard enough that I need to *run* from you. Get a grip."

First, Rashad scoffed. Then, he openly laughed as he moved to the side, extended his arm in invitation for me to pass. I did, without even tossing him a glance, but the closer I got to his front door, the more pissed off I got.

I turned on my heels, intending to go back to the studio, but instead I walked right into Rashad's chest. I had *not* expected him to be right behind me. Steadying myself quickly, I gave a haughty sniff before launching into a tirade. "You know what, guys like you really make me sick. There was a moment there, where I really thought you *might* be okay, but then you open your mouth to say some of the *stupidest* shit, like there's no way I'd be able to resist you if we stayed in the same room. Screw you, screw your little head games. You're just like your damned homeboy!"

"What are you talking about, B? What *homeboy*?"

"Drew!" I spat back, chest heaving. "And don't call me B, we're not friends, you don't get to call me by a nickname.

Rashad's face balled up in confusion. "*Drew*? I don't have a homeboy named... wait a minute... are you talking about Drew Randle?"

"You *know* that's who I'm talking about."

He backed up, shaking his head. "Man, get outta here, I don't kick it with that dude."

"Whatever, Rashad."

"Nah," he said, stepping forward again. "It's *not* whatever. I need this to be clear: I know him, but Drew Randle is *not* my homeboy, I *don't* kick it with him, and I *don't* do the type of shit that he does. I do *not* fuck with Drew. That's not my style." He wasn't exactly yelling at me, but his voice was raised, his words emphatic as he spoke. More importantly... there was a sincerity in his eyes that I'd *never* seen in the man I'd accused him of being close with. I knew *right* then that Drew had lied about their relationship, and that I'd misjudged Rashad. No way he'd be denying it *this* hard if he and Drew were anything alike.

Outside of *my* experience with Drew, I knew exactly why Rashad didn't want to be associated with him. Drew had long held the reputation of a "bad boy" photographer, but over the last couple of years — really since our for real, *final* break up, he'd been progressively worse. Drinking, fighting, lewd acts in public, and there were rumors of "misconduct" — meaning harassment — with underage models. He was a great photographer, but his reputation among the reputable magazines was going down the tank. I couldn't blame Rashad for not wanting to be linked to him.

"Hold up," Rashad said, cupping his elbow with one hand, and using the free ones to tap his chin. He stared at me for a short moment, like he was figuring something out, then asked, "Is *Drew* the one you—"

"No." I shook my head. "And it doesn't matter anyway. That's not your homeboy, fine. It doesn't change the fact that you're an asshole, and you get on my goddamned nerves."

His expression shifted from concerned curiosity to a smirk. "You know why I get under your skin, so bad, right?"

"I know why you *think* you get under my skin. I pegged *that* the first night, remember? Arrogant, spoiled—"

"And *too handsome for my own good*," he said, that smirk spreading into a full on smile. "How could I forget the *first* time you admitted you wanted me?"

I crumpled my face into a scowl. "*First* time? *Wanted* you? Are you serious?"

"Dead serious, baby." He stepped closer again, and I stepped back, meeting quite suddenly with the hallway wall behind me. "First time was the night at UG. Second time was at Sugar&Spice. Tell the truth… if Cameron hadn't said anything we'd probably still be pressed together right now."

"Oh *please*."

"So I'm lying? You wouldn't have hugged me?"

"I… I… *ugh*," I groaned. "Get out of my way, so I can leave."

Laughing, he stepped to the side and I shoved past him, heading for the door.

"There she goes again, running away," he called after me, and even though I *knew* what he was doing, *knew* I should keep walking, I turned around again.

"What is your issue?!"

He shook his head, tossing his hands up in the air. "*I*

don't have one. *Your* issue is that you want me. That's why I bother you so much. Live a little, Bianca. *Let yourself have me,*" he chuckled, sauntering up to me from down the hall.

"You are *so* full of yourself."

"You don't want me?"

I tipped my head back, looking up at him as he got in my personal space again, all delicious brown skin and muscles. But I ignored all that, and swallowed hard. *"I don't want you."*

"Then *why*," he said, backing me into yet another wall. "Are you still here, Bianca? Nothing, nobody, is stopping you from leaving... unless that's not what you wanna do."

I... couldn't breathe, let alone *respond* to the fact that Rashad's hand was at my waist now. He was *touching* me, but I quickly deemed it not intimate, because the thin fabric of my shirt was between us. But then... his warm palm was against my bare skin, and the way he dug his fingers into flesh surely wasn't *not* intimate. Then his hand was on my face, cupping my chin, slipping under my collar to caress my neck, and he was lowering his face to brush my lips with his.

"Tell that lie again, B." His voice was low, husky as he pushed my jacket from my shoulders, letting it fall to the ground in a heap around my feet. My brain hadn't even started processing a response before his mouth was on mine, gently tugging my bottom lip between his teeth before he sucked it, nipped it again, then kissed away the sting.

"*Say it*," he murmured against my lips. But how the hell

was I supposed to think straight when his nimble fingers were making quick work of my buttons, and what seemed to be less than a second later, I was down to my bra? "Say it, Bianca," he insisted. "Tell me you don't wanna be here. Tell me you wanna leave. Tell me you want me to stop touching you, and I will. I don't wanna do anything you don't wanna do, so... just *tell* me. I'm listening."

But... his hands were on my breasts, and his mouth was on my neck, and his tongue was... "*Oh my God,*" I whimpered as his tongue connected with my ear, nibbling, kissing, sucking me there too. He gripped my waist, pulling me into his body as he sucked my neck. "Rashad, I...."

"Yeah?"

Suddenly his eyes were on mine, wondering, waiting to see what I was going to say or do. This was... nonsensical and I knew it. Rashad was *exactly* the wrong person to attempt a one-night stand with, but... he was right. I wanted him *so damned bad*, and I didn't even understand *why*, not when he tap danced on my nerves, but... did it even really matter?

He was single, so was I. He was grown, so was I. Yes, I was in a place where emotionally, I was anti-relationships, anti-love, but... what was a little harmless sex with someone I could barely tolerate, right? The longer I stared at Rashad without giving him an answer, the closer his fingers drifted to the button on my jeans.

I pulled my lip between my teeth, chest heaving as I weighed my options. Rashad's fingertips skimmed my waistband, and I calculated that it had been four *long* months since the last time I'd had sex, and it really wasn't an experience worth remembering. He unhooked the button, and the fact that we were kinda, sorta co-workers played in my mind. His forefinger and thumb gripped my zipper, and I thought about how unlikely he was to "catch feelings", and how *very* likely he was to practice discretion. Rashad slid the zipper down, and I felt a tiny twinge of guilt over my budding friendship with his sister. He slipped a hand into the front of my panties, and Drew's attempt to play Rashad against me came to the forefront of my thoughts. And then he moved, and the prominent bulge in his sweat pants pressed against my thighs, hard, and heavy, and… and… and…

"Do you have protection?"

Rashad grinned, then chuckled as he slid his fingers into the wet heat between my thighs, eliciting a moan from the back of my throat. He swallowed that sound with a kiss, his free hand gripping my curls, pulling my head up to expose my neck as the next target of his lips. He kissed me there as his fingers plunged deeper, faster, more insistent, and I spread my legs wider to accommodate him.

Much too soon, he pulled away, then kneeled in front of me to unzip and remove my boots, then peel my jeans down my thighs, followed by my panties. When he was standing again, he kissed me, then reached around to my back to unsnap my bra.

Naked in front of him, my face grew hot as he swept me with his eyes. It wasn't as if I hadn't been unabashedly nude in front of a man before, but… the way Rashad looked at me was … *different*. He gripped himself through his sweats, biting his lip as he looked me over once again. I bit mine too, boldly meeting his gaze as I slipped my own fingers between my legs.

Hungrily, he watched me pleasure myself until I closed my eyes, then said, "I'll be right back," his voice raspy with lust. He only seemed to be gone for a few seconds before he returned. I heard his bare footsteps padding across the hardwood floor, and opened my eyes to see him... and nothing else. His sweats were gone, and he was rolling a condom onto... a *lot* of himself. I didn't have time to panic about it before he was in front of me, no time to mentally prepare before he'd picked me up, propped me against the wall, and pressed his sheathed erection against me.

Our eyes met, and we shared a contented sigh as he pushed inside of me, slowly, little by little, until he was burrowed deep. Rashad put his face to my neck, kissing me there as he wrapped my legs around his waist. He kissed his way up to my ear, where he nibbled my earlobe and then pulled it into his mouth.

"*Ahh*," I moaned, as he pulled out swiftly, then plunged in deep, and *slow*, repeating that a few more times until I was squeezing my eyes shut, and digging my manicured nails into his back.

He chuckled against my ear. "It's good to you, huh?"

"Don't be arrogant."

"I'm not. Just asking a question… I'll save the arrogance for after I make you come."

I rolled my eyes, even though he couldn't see me with

his tongue pressed to my neck. "I don't know why you sound so sure you can make that ha—aaa—pen."

I gasped as he pushed into me deeper, pulling me away from the wall as he drove faster, harder, keeping me upright with his arms wrapped around my back.

Holy crap.

It was so good I couldn't even catch my breath, and I *knew* he couldn't keep that pace, couldn't keep me up, couldn't keep going like that, but as soon as that thought crossed my mind, it was like it spurred him on. Hot prickles of pleasure radiated from my core to my fingertips and toes then came back, forming into intense pressure that coiled around me like a spring. Tighter and tighter, as he stroked harder and faster, until I finally gave in, and… *exploded.*

I came with an intensity that snatched away what little breath I had, leaving me gasping for air as Rashad continued stroking until he released as well. We stayed like that, panting against each other until he carried me into his room, where he gently deposited me on the bed, covering me with a soft blanket.

His presence went missing, and a moment later, I heard a door — presumably the bathroom — close. I tried *not* to listen while he peed, then listened closely for the sound of him washing his hands, which thankfully came.

I couldn't even think about leaving yet, not with my legs still tingling with barely-returned feeling, but I guess that didn't matter anyway. When Rashad came out of the bathroom, he was wearing a smirk, and another condom.

He slid under the blanket with me, pressing his chest against my back as he kissed my neck.

"You think I can make that happen for you again?" he asked, gripping a handful of my ass before slipping his fingers between my thighs.

Pressing my face into the sheet, I smiled as a plan sprang to my mind. "I don't know…"

"Ohhh, so you don't believe me?" He rolled me onto my back, then positioned himself between my legs. "Then, *watch*."

"Nuh-uh," I said, sitting up. I shoved him onto his back, then climbed on top, already rolling my hips as I lowered myself onto him with a grin. "*You* watch."

five

. . .

rashad

HE *WARNED* ME.

My father *warned* me about trouble, and I... my dumb ass went skipping right into it. I *knew* Bianca was trouble, and I rolled with it anyway. Because... pretty. And passionate, and interesting, and sexy, and smart, and... damn.

Bianca wasn't trouble, nah... she was a goddamned *disaster*.

She looked so innocent though... fresh-faced and calm, her pretty little lips slightly parted as she slept. I watched her chest as it rose and fell, my hands itching to cup her rich brown breasts, mouth watered at the memory of tasting her nipples. The thigh she'd draped across my legs was pleasantly warm in my chilly apartment, and I wanted to pull the covers over us again, but... I didn't want to move.

I knew this was something I would panic about later,

but shit... I wanted to be in this moment with her. Damned if I understood *why*. I didn't... *cuddle*, I didn't *enjoy quiet moments*, I didn't let chicks sleep with me in *my* bed. Bianca stirred a little in her sleep, mumbling something unintelligible as she wrapped herself tighter around me, pushing the apex of her thighs against my leg.

Okay.

So maybe I *did* cuddle.

Shit.

I didn't even know Bianca well enough for being with her like this to feel like *anything,* let alone for it to feel so damned *right*. But... according to Pops, that's what trouble did.

In the wee hours of the morning, she finally opened her eyes, staring at me for a long moment as her brain took a few moments to come alive. Her eyes widened with recognition, and her breath caught in her throat as her gaze traveled from my face to my body, naked and pressed against hers.

What is she gonna do, I wondered. If I had to guess, she was about to freak out. She would curse, call me everything except my name, then storm out with her clothes on, but askew.

I just had to wait, watch, and hopefully be turned off by her antics.

"Well," she said, sitting up and stretching her arms wide. "That was... fun, right?"

I shrugged at her, but she kept looking at me,

expectantly, like she was waiting for an answer. "Uhh...
yeah."

She scooted to the edge of the bed and stood, stretching
again, with her nude, magnificent body on full display.

Damn she's sexy.

When she was done stretching, she padded into the
bathroom and closed the door, and ten minutes later she was
back, with her hair looking much less wild, and her face a little
more awake. Bianca said nothing as she left the bedroom, and
when a couple of minutes passed without her coming back, I
followed her out to my living room. I found her neatly dressed,
perched on the end of the couch as she put on her boots, and
she barely looked up when she heard me enter the room.

I really wasn't sure how to feel about that.

She finished with her boots, slipped into her jacket, then
stood, and *then* she really looked my way. "So... you'll let
me know if everything was good with the video?" she
asked, checking her little wristlet-purse-thingy for her cell
phone and keys.

"Uhh... yeah."

"Cool." Bianca stepped toward the door, then turned
back, her eyes traveling over my body until they landed on
my dick, which was at full attention, despite the fact that I
was *really* fucking confused. She lifted a hand to her neck,
rubbing absently until she gave a slight shake of her head
and looked away, returning her gaze to my face. "So... I'm
gonna head home. I'll see you around."

"Uhh... yeah."

A second later she was gone, and that was the moment I realized that Bianca Bailey wasn't trouble, or a disaster... she was a *catastrophe*.

Seriously!

How the *fuck* did I go from filming her bio, to realizing that I wasn't imagining the fact that she wanted me, to planning to *wear her out*, to getting my *damned* self worn out, to feeling like the piece-of-ass-on-the-side that didn't get invited to dinner?!

Seriously.

What. The. Fuck?!

I stood there for the longest time after she left, trying to figure out what the hell my life was about anymore, when I was actually disappointed that a casual sex encounter had ended without any hassle. Shit was *baffling* to me.

But... luckily I had work to do, so I didn't really have to think about that. I spent the next two days editing bios for each blogger's page, then put together a director's cut of all the bios together, which I knew Cameron would wanna see.

I put off editing Bianca's video for last. For one, there was that whole out of sight, out of mind thing, not that *that* shit actually worked. But mostly, it was because it pissed me off to hear her talk about Drew's stupid ass.

Ugh.

It made me sick to my stomach to think about Bianca comparing me to him, and even sicker to know she'd been a victim of his bullshit. It never surprised me anymore to hear negative shit about that dude.

At first, I thought he was cool. We met at a photography conference where he was running a session, and we vibed. He was only a year or so older than me, but I looked up to his work. Over that weekend, we kicked it hard. Loud music, liquor, women... we lived it up. Afterwards, we kept in touch, partied together whenever we happened to be in the same city.

But then... things started popping up about trashed hotel rooms, rumors of drug use, stuff like that, and I had to pull back. Drew was cool, but not enough that I was gonna put *my* reputation on the line. And then it got worse, with arrests, pictures of him puking and passing out all over social media, and what completely killed it for me: whispers of him groping, inappropriate touching, and much, *much* more with models, some of whom were only 16-17 years old. *That* was some shit I absolutely didn't get down with, and wasn't trying to be linked to.

So... if he was doing all of that, it really came as no surprise to me that he would be borderline abusive. I didn't know for sure when he and Bianca broke up, but I'd known Drew for the last three years, and never even got an inkling that he *had* a main girl.

In any case, the sorrow in Bianca's eyes when she talked about him made my chest hurt, but there was hope there too. The more I learned about Bianca, the more I wanted to know. She wasn't just a pretty girl who knew how to put together an outfit, there was real meaning behind what she did, and a passion for others.

She was... *seriously* dope.

Which was… a problem.

The next time Bianca and I were in the same room was the following Wednesday at Sugar&Spice. Cameron had set up a meeting for the local bloggers, while the others teleconferenced in, to watch the Director's cut I'd given her of the bios.

I hadn't seen Bianca, hadn't heard from her, which was, in itself, a surprise. When I had *incredible* sex with somebody, it happened more than once, meaning more than just that night. We got it in for days, sometimes *weeks*.

Bianca was messing up a *working* strategy.

No calls, no texts, no nothing, and she walked right past me to get to her seat in the conference room. I leaned back in my chair and turned, watching the curve of her hips and the swell of her ass in her slim fitting jeans as she moved.

Damn she looks good, I thought as she rounded the edge of the table. She looked back in my direction, and her face brightened into a bit of a smile. I was about to smile back when I realized she was looking over my head, and I turned to see wack-ass Kieran walking into the room, grinning like he'd won the damned lotto.

I sucked my teeth as he approached her, pulling her into a hug that was honestly innocent, but… fuck that. I shook my head at *that* scene, then turned my chair back toward the table, where I felt eyes on me. I looked up, and my gaze met Raisa's.

She was wearing a smug little grin as she cut her eyes in the direction of Kieran and Bianca, who were still talking, then turned back to me and stuck out her tongue. A second later, my phone vibrated in my pocket, and I pulled it out to see a text from her.

"That's what you get for being mean to her. — Twin."

I scoffed, then shook my head as I tapped out a message. *"What you talking about?"*

"Shad, please. It burns you up to see her be friendly with Kieran doesn't it? You like her don't you? — Twin."

"And don't even send me the lie you were about to type out. Maybe if you stop pushing her down on the playground, there could be something there. — Twin."

"Nothing to lie about. Ain't nothing going on between me and Bianca. Nobody thinking about her like that."

Take that.

I sent her the lie *anyway*, though we both knew what it really was. Raisa always *knew* when it came to me and the opposite sex. She read my chemistry with the women around me like it was her profession, and although I hated to admit it... she'd never been wrong. It had been a *long* time since she pushed the issue with any girl for me... and it honestly freaked me out that her first endorsement in years was Bianca.

I stuck my phone back in my pocket, and tried not to let it bother me that when Bianca sat down beside Raisa, Kieran sat on her other side, getting all up in her personal space to speak something into her ear. Granted, Bianca *did* ease away from him, but still. When did *they* get so cozy?

I felt Raisa's eyes on me again so I looked up, and when our gaze met, she motioned at her phone. I fished mine from my pocket again, noticing that she'd sent another message.

"Well since you *don't* like her, it probably *won't* make you feel any better to know that she's not into Kieran like that. — Twin."

Shaking my head, I chuckled, then glanced up at Raisa with a smile. She returned it with one of her own, accompanied by a wink as Cameron, Aubrey, and Denise entered the room. A few minutes later, the lights went low, and everybody sat back and watched as the bios started.

I'd already seen them all several times, so instead of looking at *that* again, I observed Bianca. She smiled and laughed along with Raisa as they watched, occasionally moving to say something in the other's ear. When her video came up, Bianca visibly stiffened, then slowly, furtively, she flicked her eyes in my direction. I wondered if, like me, the sight of herself on screen had brought about memories of what happened after the video ended.

Our eyes met, just for a second before she looked away, turning her attention back to the screen. Bianca chewed nervously at her bottom lip as she watched herself respond to my questions, then covered her face with her hands as her on-screen-self blushed when I asked about her love life. The whole room laughed, except for Kieran, who frowned up like something smelled bad, then glanced back at me like he had a problem.

The fuck?

My mouth curled into a sneer and he quickly fixed his face, turning away as quickly as he'd turned his wack ass around. Raisa put her hand on Bianca's shoulder when she started talking about her message of self-worth, then leaned forward to say something in her ear. When Bianca turned back to the screen, I caught a glimpse of the glossiness in her eyes, and almost wondered if I'd made a mistake in including that part. It *was* pretty personal... what if she regretted giving it?

I kept my gaze on Bianca as the video ended, and before the lights came back up, she turned to me, giving me the tiniest hint of a smile of reassurance. The room turned into a buzz of activity after that, and there was really no reason for me to stay. I stood, intending to say goodbye to Raisa, who was on the far end of the room, past the point where Bianca was standing talking to Kieran and Asha.

Bianca's back was to me, but Kieran looked up as I approached. He stepped closer to her, giving me a look that was distinctly territorial, and... suddenly I wasn't so ready to go home.

Because... *what?*

I walked right up, looking between them as the conversation lulled, undoubtedly because of my presence. "What are we talking about over here?" I asked, casually pushing my hands into the pockets of my jeans, as if I'd always been a part of the conversation. "Kieran isn't over here boring you ladies with obscure sports stats is he?"

Asha snickered, and Bianca's eyes went wide as she looked away — an affirmative, yet nonverbal answer to my question. I chuckled as I clapped Kieran on the shoulder, *maybe* a little harder than I had to. "I'm kidding man. I think it's really cool that you're able to rattle off such... archaic... information, just like that. "

"Rashad."

Damn.

I glanced behind me to see Cameron standing there, wearing an unreadable expression. "I need to see you," she said, motioning with her head for me to trail her. She didn't wait for me, just started moving, and I really didn't have much choice other than to follow as she led me to an empty corner of the room.

"What's up, boss lady?" I asked, looking over Cameron's shoulder at Bianca as she and Kieran resumed conversation. She looked bored as hell.

"I wanted to tell you that you did a really wonderful job with those bios. Thank you for handling that for me. I'm really pleased with how well you're taking on your new responsibility."

I nodded absently, cursing in my head as Kieran *finally* left Bianca and Asha. Raisa joined them shortly after.

"Are you listening to me, Rashad?" Cameron asked, reaching up to cup my face, pulling it down so I was looking at her. "Or are you too busy admiring the pretty fashion blogger for your *boss* to pay you a compliment?"

She lifted an eyebrow at me as she released her grip on my face, then crossed her arms over her chest.

I scrubbed a hand over my head as I groaned. "Sorry Cam. It's—"

"You slept with her and messed around and got yourself sprung." She shook her head, waving a hand in front me.

"It's *all* over your face. I've been around a little bit longer than you, I know that look *well*."

Laughing, I leaned into the wall behind me. "Ain't nobody *sprung*, come on now. I can't innocently admire a beautiful woman?"

"*You*?" Cameron laughed. "*No*. It's never *just* innocent admiration with you, and we both know that. Besides... the chemistry is obvious in the video. The way she responded to you, how open she was... how hard she blushed when you asked about her love life."

I sucked my teeth. "You're blowing smoke, nothing had even happened yet when we were filming the— *shit*."

"Mmhmm." Cameron pressed her lips together to suppress a smile. "So it happened *after*. I knew better than to send that girl to your apartment. Rashad... please, don't let your dick get you into something you brain can't get you out of."

"So... are you saying I'm in trouble?" I asked, lowering my brow.

Cameron shrugged. "With *me*? Not at all. Y'all are grown. As long as it doesn't affect me, my business, or your ability to do your job, you're free to do what you want, but I *swear to God*, I will *choke* you if you make me look bad. Got it?"

I gave her a mock salute. "Aye-aye, boss lady."

"Mmhmm."

She gave me a last warning glance as she walked off, and when I looked up, Raisa, Asha, and Bianca were nowhere in the room.

Shit.

Even though it really wasn't my reason for sticking around — or maybe it was — I was annoyed that I'd missed an opportunity to see what was up with Bianca. If... *anything* was up with Bianca.

What was my damned problem?

When had I turned into *this* whiney ass dude, pining after a woman?

I made a mental note to call my dad, and ask how to fix whatever I'd broken in my head fooling with Bianca, then left the conference room. A vibration in my pocket notified me of an alert on my phone, and I pulled it out to check.

My eyes grew wide when I saw the newly received email from the realtor I'd contacted a few weeks before. I tapped the little envelope icon, still walking as I waited for it to load.

Mr. Martin, good news! I found a place in the price range that you gave me, and I think it will work for you and your sister. Good light, big windows, plenty of space for a workshop for her, and a studio for you. If you're still in the market, let me know. We can arrange some time for a showing.

I grinned down at the phone as I read the message again, then forwarded it to Raisa. *Hell yes* we were still interested. If the price was right, leasing space was the next step for us to owning our own businesses. The freelance thing was cool, but I wanted a studio, with a *real* dark room, Raisa wanted to teach DIY classes, and have a place to work and film videos without destroying her and Gabe's fancy apartment.

This was *perfect*.

I was skimming that email for the third time when I reached the elevators, and pale purple curls pulled my attention away from my phone. I turned off the screen, slipping it back into my pocket as I approached.

She was absorbed with her phone as well, and didn't notice me or look up until I spoke. "Bianca," I said, stepping in front of her. "Thought I'd missed you."

"Oh...." Her pierced eyebrow slowly ascending toward her hairline. "Did you need to speak to me about something?"

"Well... I...."

Shit.

I was in front of her now... what *did* I have to say?

I knew for a fact that transparency *wasn't* the move. Seriously, I wasn't about to say *Yeah, I was tryna see if I could get you back to my place*, or, *it's really throwing me for a loop that you seem so unphased.*

I scratched my head, looking around for something else to focus on before I finally brought my eyes back to her face. "I mean... I didn't have anything in particular, I guess I... wanted to see what was up with you, after the other night."

"The other night?" She angled her head to the side, confusion filling her eyes. "What about it? It was just... *sex*, right? I mean... a no strings attached thing?"

Moving my hands to my pockets, I rocked back on my

heels for a second. "Yeah, I guess. I thought… you know what, never mind."

This shit was *bananas*! I'd *never* experienced anything close to this… this… feeling of rejection? The *fuck*?

"Oh my God, *look* at you," Bianca giggled, her eyes brimming with amusement as she shook her head. "You can't even figure out what to say to me, can you?"

I scoffed, pulling my face into a scowl. "What are you talking about, B?"

She laughed harder then, lowering her phone to stick in her pocket. She ran her tongue over her lips, then smirked as she took a step closer, inclining her head to look me right in the face. "You're feeling antsy, aren't you Shad?" she asked, running her fingers over the buttons of my shirt. "Your world is all upside down, and you're confused, feeling unwanted, right? I can tell you why, if you wanna know."

What the hell…

"Tell me," I said, narrowing my eyes as her hands reached up to straighten my collar.

She gave me a slick, self-satisfied smile, then pushed herself up on her toes to speak into my ear. "I broke your stupid ass logic."

Bianca lowered herself back onto her heels, looking incredibly smug as she turned toward the elevator and moved her finger toward the call button.

"Hold on a second now." I stepped in front of her, intercepting her summoning of the elevator. "Explain what you mean."

She propped her elbow in one hand, chin in the other. "Well... when we first met, you were arguing the point that women were liars. That we *claimed* we could have good sex without falling in love, or getting sprung, catching feelings, whatever. Well... *we* had good sex, and yet... here I am... not in love. Go figure."

She gave me a *big* grin after that, and it took a second before I could even respond. "So... you not calling or anything, barely speaking when you saw me today... that was all to prove a point? You realize that taints the result of your experiment, right?"

"*Wrong*," she laughed. "Rashad, I wouldn't have called you anyway. But look at *you*, it's barely been three days and you're walking around here scowling, no flirting, nothing. I messed your head *all* up, didn't I? Gave it to you good and *you* caught yourself a little case of the feelings, the very same thing you accused women of doing. Would you *look at that*!?"

I opened my mouth to respond, but then... I let out a bark of laughter as I realized... goddamn... she was *right*. "Aiight, B. So what? I like you," I admitted, shrugging. "What's so wrong with that?"

"*Nothing*," she laughed, shaking her head. The next moment, her good mood, seemingly brought on by laughter at my expense, had sobered. "But... Rashad, what I told you that night at your place is the truth. I'm... not available."

I scratched my jaw. No way she was serious. "At all?"

She stared at me for a long moment, her lip pulled

between her teeth as she contemplated her answer. Finally, she reached past me to press the call button on the elevator, then looked up at me again. "Not available *at all…* for anything more than what we did the other night."

I started to speak, then stopped as the elevator came to a halt on our floor. Bianca stepped into the empty unit, and I started to follow, but she held up a hand, shaking her head.

"Not now… but we'll talk."

We held eye contact until the doors closed, and yet another unfamiliar feeling sparked in my stomach. My head was swimming with new information to process, and the compelling need to figure out why I was so caught up in Bianca. And that wasn't even including the implications of that *last* little part of the conversation. I didn't know *what* the hell I was doing when it came to her.

I was supposed to be backpedaling *away* from trouble, not sprinting into it.

six

. . .

bianca

"*SHH. I HIDING.*"

I grinned as my three-year old niece crawled into my
bed and burrowed herself under the covers, after barging
her way through my bedroom door.

A few seconds later, Lauren stopped in my doorway and
looked around, her eyes landing on the child-sized lump
beside me under the comforter. Her shoulders dropped, and
she smiled as she stepped inside, sitting down at the edge
of the bed.

"Well, B. It looks like we lost Harper. I don't know how
Mrs. Marshmallow Puff is gonna take it, but I guess I'll go
break the news. She was just telling me how she was *so* sad,
and couldn't sleep without Harper. This is *really* gonna
break her sweet little marshmallow heart. How awful for
her."

"*Waiiiit*," Harper wailed, flipping the covers from over her head and flinging herself into her mother's arms. "Mommy, is Mrs. Marshmallow Puff gonna cry?"

I covered my hand with my mouth, torn between laughing and crying at the anguish in Harper's adorable voice. Lauren cut her eyes in my direction, and I could tell she was suppressing her own smile.

"Well baby, she *might*. It's bed time, and when we couldn't find you, she was really upset. She's waiting for you in the bed, so I think you'd better go keep her company. And besides... your auntie was kind enough to let us come and spend the weekend with her... we probably should, at some point, go to sleep. What do you think?"

Harper nodded, her eyes big, expression solemn as she climbed out of her mother's lap. "Goodnight Auntie Bee!" she chirped, blowing me a clumsy kiss as she hurried out of the room in her unicorn slippers.

"Goodnight Sweet Pea," I called after her, grinning at Lauren as I shook my head. "You're gonna eventually have to stop lying to that girl to get her to go to sleep. That damn stuffed marshmallow kitten, or whatever that thing is, isn't gonna work forever."

Blowing out a sigh, Lauren fell back on the bed, arms stretched wide. "I know, I know. But... it works for *now*, and it's the only thing that does. It's not broken, so I'm not about to try to fix it."

Chuckling, I let my tablet slip from my lap as I moved so that I was beside Lauren on the bed, rolling over so that I was on my stomach, and propped on my elbows. "Does she sleep for Mrs. Tanya?"

"Girl, of *course* she sleeps for grandma, but you know how *that* goes." She let out another sigh, then draped her hands behind her head like a pillow. "She basically lives with them, you know? So it makes sense that *their* routine is *the* routine. Mommy is the novelty around here."

I rolled my eyes. "Don't say shit like that, Lauren."

"It's the *truth*," she scoffed. "Am I lying?"

Moving my weight to one elbow, I reached over and pinched her in the fleshy part of her arm. "For real, sis. Cut it out."

She sucked her teeth and smacked away my hand after a loud *ouch*, but didn't say anything else. Her pretty face, almost a duplicate of mine, sans the piercings, was serene, but I knew my sister well enough to know that her head was swirling with self doubt.

At only nineteen, Lauren was honestly one of the dopest young women I knew. She'd had Harper at sixteen, but still managed to graduate top of her class, and was in college now on straight scholarships. Harper split time between her grandparents while Lauren was off at a much better school than *any* of the locals, but every long weekend, spring break, summer break, whatever time she could, whenever she could afford it, Lauren flew back to be with her daughter. As far as I could tell, she didn't party, barely socialized. She held down her work study job, and prided herself on straight A's. According to her, she owed it to Harper.

Suddenly, she sat up, turning to me with a smile. "Okay. Enough of that... what's going on with you? What are *you* gonna be doing this weekend?"

I laughed at her clear distinction that my plans would be separate from the ones she had with Harper, even though they were staying with me for the next few days. There was some huge kid's event happening, the kind that required long hours in teeming crowds of loud, sticky children.

Hard pass on that.

"Well, while you and Harper are in the land of germs, animated characters, and junk food, *I* will be catching up on stuff for LotL. I'm supposed to be filming my first exclusive segment for Sugar&Spice, and I can't quite decide what I want to do."

Lauren playfully pushed my shoulder. "Sounds like somebody is nervous."

"Nervous isn't the word. *Terrified* is more like it. Making sure the topic is interesting, making sure *I* don't come across as boring, or bland, and then... there's the fact that I'm supposed to be working with Rashad on this."

She sucked in a slow breath, then pulled her face into a slight grimace. I'd told her *everything* about Rashad and I, so she knew how that could become even *more* awkward than it already was. I hadn't seen him in over a week, since our little discussion in front of the elevator, so I hadn't — at least not *yet* — been forced to acknowledge that I'd essentially opened the door for us to...

To do *what* exactly?

Friends with benefits wasn't quite right, since he and I

weren't exactly friends. I wouldn't call it *dating*, because I didn't date, not anybody, and certainly not *him*. *Lovers* sounded too formal, and implied that he and I were *in love*, which was the furthest thing from the truth. And besides all of that, we hadn't even—

"So, have you two swiped your brand new *cutty buddy* passes yet?"

I lifted an eyebrow.

Cutty buddy?

"No, not yet."

She smacked her teeth. "And *why* not?"

"It's... complicated," I said, shrugging.

Lauren shook her head as she lowered herself beside me on the bed, mimicking my position. "No, big sister. It's *not*. That's the appeal, right?"

I pressed my lips together, dropping my head onto the comforter. She *did* have a point. Despite Rashad's self-imposed freak out over the little game I'd played with him, I knew he didn't *really* have romantic feelings for me. It wasn't his style. He wanted me precisely because I *didn't* want him... at least not in a *let's meet parents and talk about our future* kinda way. In reality, we wanted the same things... I think.

Good sex, with no strings, with someone who understood discretion. And it didn't hurt to find it with someone whose company you enjoyed — and although I was loathe to admit it, I *did* enjoy Rashad's company, in a strange way. Honestly... it could work as an ideal situation. Sex, occasional conversation, and if or when we got sick of each other, we could simply... move on. No fuss, no headache, no... heartache.

"Yeah," I said. "That *is* the appeal. I'll have to talk to him about STD testing, and we'll have to... set some ground rules, I guess." I stopped, frowning a little. "Wait though... what on earth does this have to do with my concern about filming the segment?"

Lauren's eyes widened, like she'd just gotten caught. "Um... *nothing*," she giggled. "I was curious. I googled him, you know? That man is *fiiine.*"

"Ohh, I *know*," I groaned, turning on to my back. I was, quite frankly, *embarrassed* by the amount of time I'd spent thinking about that night in his apartment. Remembering how *delicious* he felt inside of me, the skill of his fingers, the heat of his mouth, the strength of his hands gripping my ass as I rode him, the firm comfort of his body as I fell asleep against him after, it was all so... *glorious.* "But we've gotta focus."

"On *what*, Bianca? What are you worried about? In that bio video, it seemed like you two had a great vibe. Is it even possible to be awkward around someone you're having great sex with?"

That elicited *another* heavy sigh. Because when I thought about it... I'd *never* felt awkward around Rashad. Pissed off, sure. Awkward? *Not.*

"That may not be a good thing," I said, raking my fingers along my scalp. "That *vibe* during the filming of the bio is how we ended up screwing each other's brains out."

Lauren laughed, dropping down to lay on top of her

hands. "Okay, so... something *public* then. With people around. Since it's a new segment, take him thrifting with you. You haven't even been since you moved up here, have you?"

"I haven't," I agreed. "And that's an awesome idea. I'll have to call the store ahead of time to get permission, but it could be a really cool video, especially with someone *else* doing the filming."

Pushing herself up from the bed, Lauren shot me a smile. "Okay then, there you go. The Lauren Bailey idea factory will send you an invoice."

"Oh whatever," I said as she stood. "I know your behind has already been in my closet and packed a bag."

She lifted a hand to her chest, feigning offense. "*Moi*? How dare you accuse me of such a thi—"

"Bye Lauren," I laughed, grabbing my pillow to toss at her head.

She easily dodged it, then moved to the doorway, staring at me for a second with a grin.

"What's up with you and this creepy ass look? Why you smiling at me?"

She shrugged. "I don't know, I'm... I'm happy for you, sis. Messing around with Drew... it was kinda like I lost you for that last year or so. I *needed* you, when I was pregnant, and scared, but you were dealing with your own stuff with *him*." Her voice was heavy with emotion, and I started to get up, but she waved for me to sit back down. "I'm not trying to get all emotional or anything, but for the last year... it's been almost like the old Bianca is back." She stopped again, her mouth spreading into a wicked grin. "Maybe your *cutty buddy* can give you what you need to come all the way back. I've missed you, B."

I swallowed hard, trying to quell the lump in my throat as tears sprang to my eyes. "I love you, Lau."

"I love you too." She smiled, then closed the door behind her as she went to climb into bed with Harper, and I sat back in my pillows, frantically wiping my eyes.

I *hated* thinking about not being there for my sister when she needed me, but if I couldn't promise her anything else, *that* shit would never happen again. My family were the ones who'd never shown me anything but love and compassion. Nothing mattered more than them.

But… I couldn't think about that. I pushed it from my mind before I turned myself into a mess of tears, then started writing down notes for my segment. By the time I took a break, three hours had passed, and it was well after one in the morning. Lauren and Harper were both asleep, so I went back to my tablet, to check the comments on my YouTube channel and blog.

I'd posted about the internship on my website, and was still receiving a lot of positive messages — especially about that *tiny* little exchange in the bio, between me and Rashad. Somehow, an interaction that took less than twenty seconds had people going wild. On the Sugar&Spice website, there was even a comment string, thirty messages long, speculating about whether or not I was sleeping with Rashad.

Which, of course, made me think about Rashad.

I got up and took an extra-long shower that I didn't need, because I'd already done so earlier. *This* shower included an unemotional orgasm from the jet spray on my removable showerhead, which did nothing but heighten my frustration. I dried off, lotioned, put on something comfortable for sleep, then glanced over at my phone. Before I could second-guess it, I scooped it up from the nightstand and sent Rashad a text.

"Hey."

I bit the inside of my cheek.

Really articulate, Bianca. Super duper eloquent.

I tossed the phone into my lap and turned on the TV, but didn't watch. I was too busy glancing down at my phone every two seconds, waiting on Rashad to respond.

"Who is this? – R. Martin." Was the response that finally came, and I scowled so hard at those words it made my head hurt. Because... what the hell? He hadn't even bothered to actually save my number? I was tapping away, ready to send back a scathing reply when another message came through.

"I'm playin'. What's up B?"

I was ashamed of how relieved I felt to see that next message come up on the screen. I carefully deleted what I'd written, then made myself wait a few minutes to respond, since he wanted to joke around.

"Not funny." I sent back, and moments later, *"Oh, so you're the only one who can play head games? – R. Martin."* flashed on my screen.

"Damn right."

"I see. – R. Martin."

"So what's up? You need something? – R. Martin."

Yes…

"No. Just… bored. What are you doing up? Just getting in?"

"Nah. I was actually asleep. You should send me a picture to make up for waking me up when you don't even want shit. – R. Martin."

I rolled my eyes at his words, then sat up, looking at myself in the dresser mirror across the room. Not like sending a man a picture of yourself was a foreign concept, but I knew he wasn't talking about a standard selfie. Still… I considered it.

"You send me one first."

I spent several long minutes wondering if he was gonna do it. I was about to send a follow-up text as a taunt when another message from him came through.

A picture.

I tapped to open the picture, then turned the phone around, angling my head to try to figure it out. I could see Rashad's handsome face, biting his lip as he looked down at the camera, but I couldn't figure out what was going on with the crazy angle of his arm, why it looked so skinny compared to his other arm, which I could also see in the picture, *or* why that was the focus. I turned the phone around one last time, then dropped it into my lap, clapping a hand over my mouth as understanding swept me.

Ohhhhhhhhh.

Skinny for an arm, but *perfect* for a dick.

And then, I started laughing, because Rashad was the *only* person I could imagine doing something as silly as *this*. The camera angle was from below, which meant he'd put his phone down on something, probably his bathroom counter, set the timer, and then stood over it, looking down to take the picture.

And the whole thing didn't even fit in the frame.

Jesus.

I clenched my thighs together as I remembered *that night.*

Taking a deep breath, I picked up the phone again and backed out of the fullscreen view of the picture. Rashad had sent another message.

"Don't be over there playing with yourself because of my picture... unless you're gonna let me watch. Then you can play away. – R. Martin."

"Nasty ass."

"Damned right. Now where is my picture? – R. Martin."

I tossed my head back against my pillows, then sighed heavily as I turned on my bedside lamp. Lifting my phone, I went into my camera app, tugged down my tank top enough to show some cleavage — no more than I wear out of the house on a normal day anyway — then took a mildly suggestive selfie and hit "send".

Moments later, he responded back. *"You really are gorgeous, B. – R. Martin."*

I smiled at his words until a second, then *third* message came through. *"Aiight now quit playing, gone and pull that shirt off. – R. Martin."*

"Please. 0:-) – R. Martin."

I laughed at the sheer *audacity* of him sending me an angel/halo emoji while campaigning for nude pictures of my breasts, then sent him a response. **"No can do. What if you decide to play "guess the titties" with your friends? Next thing I know, my breasts are on the internet, and I think I'll hard pass on that possibility."**

"I'm really offended that you think I would share. I'm a photographer, baby. I would never distribute your work without proper permission and or attribution. I appreciate all forms of artistry... especially the "art of the nude". Consider me a curator. – R. Martin."

"I consider you a damned fool. And why is your dick hard in the middle of night anyway?"

"Cause I'm talking to you. Why wouldn't it be hard? – R. Martin."

"But we aren't talking, we're texting."

"So... maybe you should hit that call button then. – R. Martin."

Hmm.

Maybe your cutty buddy can give you what you need to come all the way back.

Maybe... I *should* hit the call button. Because... why the heck not?

So... I *did*.

When Rashad answered, with a simple "What's up, B?", with his voice all low, and raspy with sleep, moisture pooled between my thighs, because... *sexy*.

"Nothing. You're the one who said I should I call."

He chuckled, and *that* sent a fresh wave of arousal over my skin. "Oh, you're following instructions now or something? You're into that?"

"What? *No*," I said, wrinkling my nose. "I meant that the phone call was *your* suggestion, so... you tell *me* what's up."

"*You're* what's up. Sounding all sexy at two in the morning, like you're about to say some nasty shit to me while I jack off. Which... I'm down with, by the way."

I rolled over onto my side, shaking my head as I held the phone against my ear. "Nasty ass."

"You said that already."

"And I'm saying it again."

"Yeah, well... say something else. Tell me something good. What else you got on besides that little tank top?"

I glanced down at my boy short panties, then grinned as I spoke. "Well... I'm wearing the biggest, oldest, baggiest pair of *that time of the month* panties I own. And big thick fuzzy socks. And oh, I *can't* forget my leopard print fleece pajama panties. I should send a picture, I look *so* hot."

Rashad laughed again, and I swear it was as potent to me as his touch, rippling through my chest, and making me feel *warm*. "I've been meaning to tell you, you can't lie worth shit Bianca. That doesn't even sound like you. I bet you're in some type of itty bitty panties. Yeah... tank and panties sounds like Bianca."

"So you think you know Bianca?"

There was a short pause, then a puff of air as he scoffed. "I don't think there's a man on the planet who can say, unequivocally, that he *knows* Bianca. But I *do* know you sound sexy as hell right now on this phone, goddamn."

"Oh, *please*," I giggled. "You know, I really believe men say that to *every* woman. *Talk to me in your nighttime voice, it's so sexy.*"

"They probably do," Rashad agreed, laughing. "Cause it's the damned truth. All... well, *most* women sound sexy at this time of night, because it puts you in the mind of what we're about to do."

I gave a quick snort. "What we're about to do? Expound on that, please."

Rashad sucked his teeth. "Come on, B. You *know* what we're about to do."

"I really, *really* don't."

"Okay then." He chuckled a little. "Let me break it down. You texted me because you wanna fuck. I—"

"Wait a minute, I never said that."

"Bianca... please don't interrupt me with your blatant, filthy lies."

He said that in such a serious tone that I burst out laughing, covering my mouth to muffle the sound so I wouldn't wake up Lauren or Harper.

"Can I finish?" he asked.

"Please do," I agreed, swiping tears of laughter from my eyes.

"I'm coming to your place, and I'm gonna be inside you before the sun comes up. *That's* what's about to happen."

I think... my heart may have stopped beating, just for a second.

"And what if I say no?"

"You're not gonna say no."

"*No.*"

He chuckled. "Okay, so it's opposite day then? Aiight, well, I *won't* be there in a few minutes."

"You can't come *here*," I said quickly, sitting up. "And besides, you don't even know where I live."

"You don't know what I know," he countered. "What, you got wack-ass Kieran over there or something?"

My eyebrow went *way* up near my hairline at that. *Kieran?* He was very, *very* handsome, but... a little too clean cut and conservative for me. He liked me, and I knew that, but I got the impression there was some fetishism involved with his interest in me. Kieran was the kind of guy who would marry a nice sweet girl, with the God-given amount of holes in her face, who would give blow jobs on Tuesdays, Thursdays, and all major holidays. She would have a nice stable corporate career, or none at all, and her name would *not* be Bianca Bailey.

But... it was interesting that Rashad thought he was a threat.

"And if I *did* have him over? Then what?"

"*Then*, I'd bend you over the couch, and show him why, *exactly*, you were texting me at two in the morning instead of talking to him."

"And why is that?"

"Open your door in about three minutes and I'll show you. Again."

I stood up, pacing the floor as I continued our conversation. "Rashad, you *don't* know where I live."

"You said that already."

"I'm saying it again."

"Yeah, well... I'm saying again to you... say something else. Tell me you're gonna open the door in two minutes."

"You *can't* come here."

"You said *that* already too."

"Because I'm *serious*," I said, stopping in front of the mirror. "My sister and niece are here, sleeping."

"Then I guess you'd better be at your door waiting in one minute, when I knock."

Sudden, complete silence from my phone, followed shortly by a brief, melodic chime let me know that Rashad had hung up the phone.

Holy shit, he really is coming over here.

My first instinct was to panic, and scramble into something sexy. But, I stopped myself. He would clock that desperation in no time, and I needed to hold on to *some* power here. So... nope. Hot pink tank top, purple and white boy shorts, and lime green ankle socks. If he wanted to show up basically uninvited, he would get what he got.

Not that I was keeping exact time, but close enough to a minute after he hung up, I heard the faint sound of a light knock on my door. I *forced* myself not to rush to it, taking my time through the living room as he repeated his polite two-in-the-morning knock.

I took a deep breath before I opened the door, and the sight of him on the other side snatched that same breath away. Black hoodie, grey sweatpants, white Nikes, brown skin, and... sexiness.

He leaned against the doorframe, saying nothing as he gave my body a slow perusal with his eyes. When his gaze returned to my face, his lips perked up in a smile. "Tank and panties... just like I thought. Take 'em off."

I gave him a stern look, then stepped closer to where he was in the door. "Stop playing. Tell me how you know where I live."

"Raisa. *Duh*," he shrugged. "We shared a cab one day, and she had the car stop here because she was coming to see you. I asked which apartment and she told."

I crossed my arms. "She talks too much."

"Yeah. Tell me something I *don't* know."

"Like what?"

He gave me another one of those half-dimpled, lazy smiles, then grabbed the hem of my tank to pull me against him. "Like... what you taste like, for example." He pushed a hand between my legs, caressing me through the thin fabric of my panties. "That's one thing I don't know."

"*Rashad!*" I covered his hand with mine, stilling it against me as I glanced over my shoulder toward the door of the guest bedroom.

"What?" he asked, dipping his head to press his lips against my neck. "You're the one who came to door in this little ass tank top with your nipples poking through, and your pussy sitting *right* there in these little pretty ass panties. Like... you realize it's *right here*, don't you?"

I giggled, then moaned as he began caressing me again,

slipping his free hand underneath my shirt. "Rashad, *stop*," I whispered, reluctantly pushing him away. "Seriously… I can't do anything with my baby niece and sister here. They could hear us, or Harper could wake up at any second, walk in my room—"

"So I guess you're gonna have to lock your door tonight." He gave me a cocky smile, like that was the *obvious* answer, then lifted his hand to run his thumb over my bottom lip. "*And…* find something to put in your mouth and keep you quiet. I've got the perfect solution."

He smirked as he eased me backwards into the apartment, and I didn't resist. Gently, quietly, he closed and locked the door behind him, then in one fluid motion scooped me into his arms. I wrapped my legs around his waist as he found my neck again with his mouth, letting out a loud whimper when his tongue made contact with my skin.

He gave me a gentle swat to the ass, then murmured, "*Shh… remember?*" into my ear, before he sucked my earlobe into his mouth. I bit my lip to stifle a moan, then gave whispered directions to my bedroom. Rashad closed and locked *that* door behind him too, then tossed me onto my bed.

"Okay," he said, kneeling before me on the floor. "Truth moment."

I lifted an eyebrow, then propped myself up on my elbows. "What's up?"

With one hand on either of my legs, he spread them apart, then used them to drag me to the edge of the bed.

"What I said earlier about wanting to know what you tasted like… I *really* do intend to find that out. But — and I'm not implying *anything* — safety first."

He stared at me, eyes wide, waiting for me to catch his meaning. When I did, I smiled. *Hard.*

"Rashad… are you talking about being tested?" I asked, closing my eyes as he pressed his lips to the inside of my knee.

"*Mmhmm.*" He turned to kiss the other knee, then trailed his tongue along the inside of my thigh, and I squeezed my eyes tight.

"Did you think I would be offended by that?"

He kissed the middle seam of my panties. "Some chicks don't like it."

"Well, your desire to be disease-free is a turn on to me. You show me your most recent paperwork and I'll show you mine." I opened my eyes when Rashad's mouth left my skin, and looked down to see him giving me a confused look with a furrowed brow. "You didn't like that?"

He chuckled, shaking his head. "It was… something."

"Hater."

"Whatever." He smirked at me, then looked down again, his eyes landing right between my legs. His golden-brown irises darkened with lust, and he ran his tongue over his lips. "B…," he said, his voice raspy with lust. "Tell me you have that information handy."

I grinned, then spread my legs a little wider, propping my feet up on the bed with my knees bent. "I can email it to you. You?"

"Same. Let's make it happen."

Because I knew he was ready, and seemingly in a hurry, I took my time crawling across the bed to get to my phone. On all fours, I left my butt hiked in the air as I navigated to the password-secured folder where I kept any private documents, and sent my latest test results to his phone. Not even a few seconds later, my phone chimed with an alert from him, and the next few moments were quiet as we both perused the others' clean bill of sexual health.

I was about to turn off my screen and put my phone down when I felt Rashad behind me. Before I could turn around, he'd yanked my panties down my legs, and the next thing I felt was his hot tongue against my sensitive flesh. My thighs jerked and quivered as he devoured me like he was starved, licking and *slurping*, and using an arm around my waist to keep me from moving away. He closed his lips over my clit and sucked *hard*, flicking me with his tongue, and the room started to spin around me.

I squeezed my eyes shut as he pushed a first, then second finger inside of me, making them work as hard as his mouth and tongue. I grabbed one of my pillows, pulling it against my face and biting down to muffle the moans and cries of pleasure that I couldn't have helped if I tried. At that moment, control belonged to Rashad, and he wasn't *giving* me an orgasm. He was about to snatch it right out of my body.

He plunged his fingers deeper, and slurped harder, stroked me faster until even though my eyes were closed, I saw an explosion of colors as my body tensed, and I came...

hard. So hard that there were a couple of seconds where I wondered if the air would ever return to my lungs, and tears welled in my eyes.

I collapsed, panting, face down on the bed, listening to the soft rustling sounds of Rashad taking off his clothes. "B?" he said, planting kisses from the base of my spine to my shoulders. "Another truth moment, Gorgeous."

"Yeah?"

He pressed his lips to my ear again, then outlined it with his tongue. "Tell me you're on some type of birth control. And since I'm clear, and you're clear... I don't have to put this condom on."

"I have an IUD, Rashad." I looked at him over my shoulder as I explained. "Contraception for at least two more years. We're good."

Those words were barely out of my mouth before he buried himself inside of me, then pulled me up onto my knees with my back against his chest. Like the first time, we both let out groans of relief, but this time Rashad didn't move. He wrapped his arms around me, cupping one of my breasts as he kissed my shoulder, then mumbled, "*Goddamn, you feel so good,*" in my ear.

And so do you.

He still hadn't yet moved, but having him inside me, filling me up, was a pleasurable experience on it's own. And it *did* feel good to be skin to skin, nothing between us when he finally *did* begin to stroke. He moved slowly at first, digging deeper with every plunge until he was buried completely and our bodies felt like one. I moved with him as he a set a slow, steady rhythm that built gradually into slick, sweaty, and skin-smackingly fast. He squeezed my breasts, kissed my neck, caressed my clit as he buried himself again and again, slowing down, then speeding up, never giving me the opportunity to fully catch my breath.

I let out a halting giggle as he put his mouth to my ear, asking me if it was good. I breathlessly told him that somebody who was giving it good wouldn't have to ask, and we both laughed, cause we both knew it was bullshit. My body was too open for him, way too wet to deny that I was enjoying every second of having him inside of me.

He found a ticklish spot on the back of my neck, and I giggled over and over as he kissed me there again and again, not caring that he was breaking rhythm for the sake of making me laugh. Suddenly, he pulled out, turned me around and pushed me onto my back, and the next moment he was inside of me again.

Rashad kissed me *deeply*, slowly, using one hand at my knee to keep my thigh pressed against my breast, to keep me opened wide for him as he stroked. He pushed his tongue into my mouth and I sucked it greedily, then eased back to give him mine. I rocked my hips, thrusting upward to meet him as our tongues danced, digging my nails into his back as he pushed deeper, then deeper still.

He eased an arm under my waist, pulling me closer, kissing me harder, losing his rhythm, but this time it was because *he* was losing control. And… if *he* wasn't in control, and I wasn't either, that meant we were doing what came natural. And apparently, what came natural was sexing like we were in love, getting lost in each other's eyes as we reached ecstasy in quick succession, then laying there afterwards, breathless in each other's arms.

This was a terrible idea...

But in that moment... I simply kissed him again... then moved closer.

seven

. . .

rashad

I SHOULD BUY BIANCA A RING. *Or… a car. Or maybe a house. Yeah, definitely a house.*

That was the kinda crazy shit running through my mind as I buried my fingers in Bianca's hair, watching in awe as her head bobbed up and down in my lap. She pulled away, replacing her mouth with firm strokes of her hand as she caught her breath. Then… *shit*, she looked up, gave me a sexy little grin, then stared me right in the eyes as she stuck out her tongue and ran it around me in a slow circle before covering me with her mouth again. Licking, and sucking, and making a complete mess, which was *absolutely* the right way to do what she was doing.

She was *damned* good at what she was doing, but still… I wanted to feel *her*.

"Come 'ere," I said, dragging my hand down to caress the nape of her neck. "Ride it for me." She ignored me, bringing her hand up to caress my balls as she swallowed me so deep it made my toes cramp, and I almost came off the edge of the bed. *"What the fuck are you tryna do to me?"* I mumbled, but expected no answer as she repeated that action again, and again, and *goddamn, again,* until I lost control.

My vision went blurry, ears started ringing, body froze as she moved her hand and mouth in sync, keeping me covered until I collapsed back onto the bed, drained. I felt the depression in the mattress as Bianca climbed up beside me, wiping her mouth with the back of her hand, and even *that* was sexy. *Why* was she so damned sexy?

She straddled me with a smile. "Don't tell me you're *already* done for?" she teased, wrapping her fingers around me. I was still hard, definitely ready, and *always* down if she was. I told her to do what she felt, and she raised herself up on her knees, then slowly sank down until I was in my new favorite place: as deep in her as her body allowed.

"Gimme those lips," I said, sitting up as she began rolling her hips. I moved my mouth toward hers, but she leaned away, shaking her head.

"You don't want me to like... rinse my mouth out first or something?"

I pulled my head back, giving her a blank look. "For what?"

She stopped moving, then swallowed hard, averting her eyes like she was unsure of herself. "I mean... I just got done giving you head. I wouldn't have thought you'd be cool with me kissing you after."

"Uhh, B…You've kissed me after I've had my face buried in your pussy, right?"

She giggled. "Right."

"So what's the damn difference? You're not holding cum in your mouth so you can put it in mine or no freaky shit like that, right?"

"Ugh, Rashad!" she said, frowning. "*Absolutely* not, this isn't a damned porn!"

I chuckled, then wrapped my arms around her to pull her close. "Don't *ugh* me, that's what you're acting like was about to happen. If we can kiss after I've been down on you, we can kiss after you've gone down on me. We're *grown*. Why wouldn't that be okay?"

"Well…." She shrugged, then looked away from me again. "You're the first person I've done that for since my ex, and he always—"

"Aiight, well you can kill *that* right there. Fuck him. New rules." I grabbed her chin, turning her to face me, then leaned in close to press my forehead against hers. "When I ask for these lips…" I pulled her bottom lip into my mouth, giving it a slow suck before I released. "Or *these* lips…" I slid my free hand between us, then between her legs. "You *give me lips*… okay?"

Her eyes went glossy, wide with wonder as she stared into mine. Her nostrils flared, and… I knew right then that she was about to cry. So… I kissed her. A slow, deep kiss to reinforce my words, and when I pulled back, I asked her again. "So what are you gonna do when I ask for lips?"

This time, she bit her lip, trying to suppress a smile. "I'm... gonna give you lips."

"You sure?"

"Yeah."

"Okay, so gimme those lips right now."

She giggled, then cupped my face, giving me a juicy wet kiss right on the mouth.

"Hell yes," I said, smacking her butt. "*That's* more like it."

»——«

"So... Mr. Martin, tell me why what you do matters?"

I lifted my eyebrows at Bianca as she held her phone up, recording me with her camera. It was almost four in the morning, and were both sexed-out, but for some reason I was still there, and we were... kicking it.

She had her sheet wrapped around her nude body, and her eyes were low, but she was alert, and interested... which was *interesting*. After all of her bluster about us not being friends, and her basically intimating that she didn't even *want* to be... here she was, trying to get to know me.

"Photography matters because...." I tucked my hands behind my head, relaxing back onto her pillows. "The world deserves beautiful imagery."

Bianca moved the camera to the side so I could see her face as she smirked. "Don't you think that's a little shallow?"

I chuckled. "Okay, okay. I see what you did there, gonna use my own words against me?"

"It's only right." She held the sheet around her like I hadn't already seen, kissed, or touched every part of her as she shifted positions, then held the phone up again. "Answer the question."

"You're a hostile interviewer."

"You haven't *seen* hostile from me yet."

"You know what... you're right," I said. "You *haven't* drawn a weapon on me... yet."

"No comment."

"How does the *interviewer* not have a comment?"

Bianca pressed her lips together, then crawled toward me across the bed, no longer caring to keep herself covered. She straddled on my legs and sat down, and the moist heat between her thighs almost made me grab her at the waist and pull her a little further north, but she lifted her phone again, aiming at my face. "Will you just answer the question Shad?"

"Fine. The want — nah, the *need* — for beautiful imagery isn't shallow because it's not always about appealing to the eyes. Not that *that's* not perfectly acceptable, because it's human nature, but the evocative appeal goes beyond physical gratification. It's about connection with the emotion of the moment. Cute animals and babies make people smile. Boosts their mood. Depending on where your head is, wedding pictures can make you sad, angry, optimistic. Pictures of bodies lined up in war-torn countries makes you grateful that it's not your reality, makes you appreciate what you have. We hear about this stuff on the news, and you feel bad. You're glad it's not you, your loved ones, but you move along, go about your day. But the *pictures*... when you see it with your own eyes, it's not so easy to move on, and it makes you want to effect change.

Think about the pictures we have from the Civil Rights movement. Think about the pictures from Central High, the Little Rock Nine. Hell, the images from Ferguson, *today*. If you only *heard* people talking about it, word of mouth, you wouldn't believe that shit. But the *pictures*, the video, you can't deny it. You're forced to face the reality, forced to connect with an existence that's not your own. You see the anger, the determination to be seen as humans in the eyes of people being mistreated and abused, and it makes you wanna *do something*. You see the hatred, the disgust, the lack of desire to see us as humans in the eyes of the people doing the mistreatment, doing the abusing, and *getting away with it* because they're them, and we're us, and *that* makes you wanna do something too.

Photography is like... a language all its own, as important as music, with a soul, and a heartbeat. It's... everything."

Bianca stared at me for a long moment, like she was processing my words, and... figuring something out. Finally, she spoke. "So... sounds like it's not just about taking pictures of pretty girls, and celebrities, and glitz and glam for you."

"Yeah, it is. Cameron gave me clearance to do more... as

much as I want, really. I didn't get to go to Ferguson, but I've done a lot of traveling to the different protests, the rallies, things like that around the country."

"Why didn't you go to Ferguson?"

I groaned, then chuckled. "Believe it or not… my mom. She'd suffered a stroke a few months before it happened. It was minor, but even minor is serious, you know? I told her I was going, had already purchased the plane ticket, and she … flipped out. Swore I was gonna get myself arrested or killed, had a panic attack, and… I had to let that idea go. Dad threatened my life for stressing out his lady, so I stuck close to home for a few months. And that's when I learned my lesson to get on the damned plane first, and tell them about it after," I laughed.

"But it's good that you prioritized your mother's health. I know it hurt to not do something that was important to you though."

I nodded. "I'm not gonna lie, I was kinda pissed off. But… I don't *ever* wanna see my mother look that helpless again. My presence *there* wasn't missed. *Here* it would have been."

"So you're close to your family?" Bianca put the phone down, then lowered herself to my chest, burrowing her face into my neck. It caught me a little bit off guard, but I put my arm around and pulled her close.

I didn't mind, but *she* was usually — as if I could really make that determination when this was only our second night together — a little more… reserved. But whatever. If she was down, so was I.

"My family is *very* close. Raisa and I see our parents at least once a week, and Raisa and I see *each other* damn near every day."

"Yeah, I've heard her call you twin, so I figured you two were close."

I was about to respond when something thumped against her bedroom door, and a moment later, someone tried to turn the nob. Bianca sat up immediately, rushing out of bed to get to her dresser.

"That's my niece," she explained, pulling a tee shirt over her head. "You should probably go. I'm gonna get her and take her to the bathroom so she doesn't see you... okay?"

Bianca pulled a pair of panties, then yoga pants up to her waist, then stopped to look at me for confirmation. I quickly agreed, turning my own legs out of the bed as she unlocked the door and slipped out.

When I crept out of her bedroom a few minutes later, she was standing in the open doorway of a bathroom halfway down the hall, speaking in a soft, soothing voice *I'd* certainly never heard. She looked up, then mouthed "potty break" to me with a smile as I headed down the hall.

I was passing another closed door when it suddenly swung open. I heard a sharp, whispered *"Harper!"* before someone walked right into me, cursed, then quickly stepped back.

"Ah, shit." Bianca whispered, closing the bathroom door as she stepped into the hall. "Lauren... meet Rashad. Rashad, this is my sister, Lauren. "

I looked down to see basically a younger version of

Bianca, with thick natural hair pulled into a ponytail on top of her head. Her mouth was pulled into a sly smile as she glanced between me and Bianca, and when her eyes finally stopped on me, they said *I know exactly what you were doing with my big sister.*

"Nice to meet you, Rashad. I've heard a *lot* about you." She gave me another little once over, then walked over to the bathroom to Bianca. "I've got Harper, B. Tend to your company." She said something else, something *lower,* and obviously only intended for her sister's ears because Bianca blushed, smacking Lauren on the arm as she switched places with her.

Lauren went into the bathroom with Harper, and Bianca grabbed my wrist, pulling me toward the door. I made the small movement that put her hand in mine, an action that I knew she was trying to avoid. She gave me a *what the fuck are you doing* look, but I gripped her hand a little tighter, and she didn't pull away until we were at the door.

"So… about my segment for the website… when are you available?" she asked, unlocking and opening the door.

I shrugged. "Pretty much whenever… you wanna do it tomorrow—well, *today,* since it's morning — or Monday?"

"Let's go for Monday… I think we could both use a little rest first."

I laughed, pushing my hands into my pockets. "I wore that ass out, huh?"

Her eyes went wide, and she blushed, glancing behind her before she turned back around. "If I'm not mistaken, it was the other way around, Mr. Arrogant."

"Ahh…" I gave her a little grin, then grabbed the front of her tee shirt to pull her close. "I don't know about all of that. We can call it even, at best. But I *will* admit," I murmured, lowering my lips to hers, "that head was so good I was thinking about buying you a house, paying off some student loans, *something.*"

"You are *so* stupid," she giggled, pushing me back.

Damn she's gorgeous when she laughs.

"I'm *dead* serious, while you're laughing." I put my hands at her waist, drawing her against my body. "I'ma go ahead and roll out, but you know what I want first, right?"

Mischief sparkled in her eyes as she shook her head, then angled her face away. "Uh uh."

"Stop playing, B." I smacked her ass, gripping handfuls to lift her off her feet. "Gimme those lips, girl."

She wiggled in my arms for a few seconds before she obliged my request, giving me a slow, sweet kiss that kinda made me wanna drag her back to her bedroom, but I heard her sister and niece in the hall. I lowered her back to her feet, then pressed my lips to her forehead. "I'll see you tomorrow."

Bianca lifted her hand to touch her lips, some unreadable emotion in her eyes. "Yeah. See you tomorrow."

I left then, but I could have sworn I heard Lauren singing *Cutty Buddy* before the door swung closed behind me.

»—«

Sunday afternoons were reserved for my parents, and that wasn't an expectation — it was a *requirement*. Unless you were out of town or incapacitated, you'd better have your ass at the table when Pamela Martin pulled that cast iron skillet of cornbread out of the oven.

On the earlier end of my twenties, I'd complained, but now that I preferred real food to microwave ramen, I appreciated this time with my family. We would eat until we could barely move, and then Raisa would disappear somewhere with my mother to talk crafting, and me and Gabe would hit the man cave with my father, Theodore, where he supplied glasses of *"something to put some hair on ya chest, boy."*

This week, my grandfather was there too, and he supplied the liquor — moonshine, which he brewed himself as a throwback hobby. I caught Gabe's eye across the room and subtly shook my head. My granddad's dad was a bootlegger back in the prohibition days, and those brewing and distillery skills were passed down to him. I knew from experience that *his* moonshine wasn't a problem Gabe wanted.

"Why ya so quiet over there son?"

I looked up from my still-full tumbler to see my father eyeing me over the tops of his glasses. "No reason in particular. Just tired."

"*Tired*? From what? It's six in the evening on a Sunday,"

he said, turning to *his* father. "Boy acts like he has a real job or something. When *I* was his age—"

"I know, you were walking 28.47 miles to school, 34.35 miles back, in the snow, on a gravel road, with no shoes." I gave my dad a wide smile as Grandad and Gabe laughed, and he grinned back, chuckling too.

"Okay, you've got your little jokes, but you know your old man had a *J-O-B*. Steady paycheck, none of this *freelancing* nonsense or whatever you call it. Benefits, so you can take care of your family."

I cocked an eyebrow. "I don't *have* a family to take care of though. And besides… I *get* a steady paycheck, the magazine hired me full time. *Not* that my income wasn't consistent before. Cameron has always paid me well Pops, you know that."

"I don't know *shit*," he exclaimed, laughing after taking a swig from his drink. "All I know is that I can call your phone on any given weekday during work hours and your ass is asleep. *That's* not how you make a living. Ask your sister's fiancé!"

I glanced over at Gabe, who shrugged, giving me a sympathetic grin. This conversation happened at least once a month, and he and Raisa had been engaged for six. He wasn't witnessing this for the first time.

"This man," dad continued, "Works for the bank. *Branch Manager*. How often you get to go home and take a nap in the middle of the day Gabe?"

Gabe grimaced, the chuckled as he shook his head. "I don't get to do that at all, sir. But Rashad does his thing, he's made a name for himself in his field. And he's still young. By the time he's my age there's no telling what he'll have accomplished."

"*Thank you*, Gabe," I said pointedly, angling my head at my father as I sent Gabe a mock salute. "At least *somebody* around here respects my craft."

My future brother-in-law laughed, but said nothing else, which was typical for him. Gabe was laid back, not a talkative dude at all — a perfect balance for Raisa, who rarely stopped. Honestly, I worried for him, dealing with the bundle of energy I called my sister, but he seemed to love that about her.

At thirty-four, Gabe was seven years older than Raisa, which concerned me — and my father — at first. But... Raisa may be bubbly, however she was certainly nobody's silly, naïve girl, to be taken advantage of. It quickly became clear that Gabe liked, then loved, the hell out of her, and she felt the same. As long as that was the case, Gabe would always be cool with me.

"I've got plenty of *respect for your craft*, son. I want you to be able to take care of yourself. You and your sister, with this techno, electric, social media, blogging shit. I don't get it. Raisa's getting married, she has a husband as a backup. *Your* ass doesn't," Dad said, leaning back in his chair.

"*Whew*," I whistled. "First off, man, you know you'd better not let Little Miss Independent hear you talking about Gabe taking care of her." My dad rolled his eyes at that as I continued. "Second, I *do* take care of myself, dad, come on. I've been working since college, never asked for anything. Give me my props, bruh."

He let out a shout of laughter, clapping his hand on his knee. "*Bruh*? Okay, Rashad. I *will* give you that. You make sure it stays that way, cause I'm not taking care of any grown ass man. *Especially* one who calls me *bruh*."

"You've got my word on that, Pops. Me and Rai are getting ready to lease this space so I can have a studio, and she can have her classroom space and all of that. So I'll have *two* jobs. Is that better?"

My granddad cleared his throat, and we all turned to him. "All this talking, and the boy *still* hasn't told us why he's so tired. Must've been up all night chasing ass."

The room erupted in laughter at my expense as I shook my head. "Nah, Grandad. It's not like that."

"Ohhh, I see. So... one *particular* ass then? Tell the truth," My dad said, leaning forward in his chair.

I scoffed, then scrubbed a hand over my face. "Well... there *is* this one girl, but it's not like *that*."

"Then what is it like?" he countered.

"She's... it's.... It's more like..."

Grandad laughed, finishing off his drink. "Sounds like *trouble* to me, son. You see how he can't even get his words out?" he asked, turning to my dad as he continued to snicker. "You're how old, Rashad? Twenty six? *Hoo* boy. Found your trouble early on."

"It's *not* like that," I insisted, putting down my glass. "We're not serious, we're... not even *friends* really."

"Mmhmm." My father eyed me skeptically, crossing his

arms. "So... she has you tired, but it's not like that, you're not even friends, and it's not that serious?"

"Right. We have... an agreement. She's not looking for anything serious, neither am I. I mean... I like her, but it's not gonna go any further than that. *That's* settled."

My father, grandfather, and Gabe glanced at each, sharing knowing looks as they shook their heads. They knew I was lying to myself, *I* knew I was lying to myself. There wasn't much of a point to speaking it out loud, especially when *Bianca*, the other half of this equation, had made it clear she wasn't trying to get down like that. Unlike when other women said it, I actually *believed* Bianca. We would have our fun while it lasted, then move on. Simple as that.

Right?

"You're in for a rude awakening boy," Granddad said. "I had one with your grandmother, rest her soul. Your dad had it with Pam. Gabe... you had one with Raisa, didn't you?"

Gabe laughed. "Man, I swore I had to leave that girl alone before she drove me into a wall with all of that energy. Instead... I gave her an engagement ring. So..." he shrugged, then gave me another sympathetic grin. "You're done for, Shad. May as well accept it."

"But she's not even sweating me," I said, looking between the other three men.

"*Exactly*," they replied, in unison, then broke into another roar of laughter.

A moment later, the door opened, and my mother stuck her head in.

"There goes *trouble* right there." My dad leaned back in his chair, eyeing my mom like he wanted to snatch her clothes off right there.

She propped a hand on her hip, giving him a playful scowl. "Teddy, I've told you about calling me that. Do you guys want dessert?"

He licked his lips. "Hell yes, I want *dessert*."

"*Teddy!*" she scolded, but gave him a wink and a little smile before molding her face back into a frown. "I'm talking about the pound cake fool."

"*So am I. I'ma pound—*"

"Come on, Pops, damn!" Shaking my head, I stood, heading over to where my mom was. "I'm gonna take *mine* to go, so I can head out before you two start stripping each other. Aiight fellas." I waved to the men, then turned around, planting a kiss on my mother's cheek as she stood in the door. "I'll see you later mama."

"Okay sweetheart. Love you."

"Love you too."

I headed down to the kitchen, where I found Raisa slicing pieces of cake and wrapping them in foil. "One of those for me?" I asked, taking a seat at the counter, even though I didn't intend to stay long.

She looked up at me and rolled her eyes. "Yeah, sure." Rai picked up one of those foil-wrapped pieces and launched it at me like a baseball, smacking me in the arm as I attempted to dodge.

"What was *that* for?" I asked, retrieving it from the floor.

"You told Bianca I *gave* you her address?"

I opened my mouth, but nothing came out, and I reached up to scratch my head. "Well... uh... *technically...*"

"Mmhmm. *Maybe* you should make the amendment that you *tickled* me until I damn near peed on myself, and wouldn't let me out of the cab until I told you. And then *I* get a text asking if I really told you where you she lived."

"She was mad at you?"

Raisa dropped the knife onto the counter, then put the cover back on the cake. "No, she's not *mad*. She was asking, probably making sure you weren't some psycho who found out by following her home."

"And what did you say?"

"I told her that I told you, because I did, even though I should have ratted you out."

I stood, giving her a quick kiss on the cheek before she could move away. "Thank you sis."

"Don't thank me. Just... be careful."

I scowled. "Be careful? What, I thought you were all for it before?"

"And I still am," she nodded. "I like Bianca, a lot. I like that she doesn't fall all over herself with you, like *every* other girl you've pursued. But Shad... she's made it clear that she's not available, not looking for anything, and I know you claim the same thing, but... what I *see*, from you, is... different. I see how you look at her, how you interact with her, and... I could see you falling really hard... only to have this girl break your heart. I don't *want* to see that happen."

"And it's *not*," I shrugged. "Yes, I like her, but I know *exactly* what we're doing here. I don't have any delusions about it. I'm chilling. She's chilling. We're good."

Raisa smiled, then shook her head. "Okay little bro."

"I'll check you later Rai, aiight?"

I waved, then headed out front to my car, which I really only pulled out for the hour long drive to my parents'. I was getting ready to pull out of the driveway when I got a text. I put the car back in park and pulled out my phone, grinning when I saw Bianca's name on the screen.

Opening the message, my eyes got *big*.

Goooddamn.

Only the bottom part of her face was showing, but her lips were bright red, and she had the bottom one pulled between her teeth. The rest of the picture was just... *titties*. Her tatted arm wasn't in the picture, and I was pretty sure that was done purposely because her ink was so identifiable, but I'd been up close and personal with *those* breasts enough to know them when I saw them. And they were *beautiful*.

I put the car in gear, but kept my foot on the brake as I tapped out a response, then pulled off.

"Beautiful. So is this an invitation, or nah?"

eight

. . .

bianca

I DIDN'T KNOW how to *not* go all in. This... whatever I was doing... with me and Rashad was perfect evidence of that. I'd known Rashad a whole... what, two weeks? And yet we'd gone *all* the way there sexually — which was fine, if the goal was to be light, and breezy, and have fun, no strings, but this was... something else. Nude selfies, late night phone calls... *getting to know each other.* This was the type of thing that could *quickly* turn into a mess.

The problem was... Rashad was too damned *likable*. It would all have been so much easier if he really *was* an asshole, or if his arrogance really were as misplaced or over the top as it really seemed. Instead, he was... *cool.* Charming. Sexy as hell. Attentive in bed. Not an idiot. And he made me laugh. He made me laugh so, *so* much, which was something I didn't realize I needed.

He... would kinda make a perfect boyfriend.

You know… if he was looking for something like that. With somebody else who was looking for something like that.

Alas, that wasn't the case for either of us, which was a little fact I should probably keep in mind before I sent another sexy picture. But… I'd put on lipstick for this one, and my boobs looked great in it, so I went ahead and pressed send.

A few minutes later, I got Rashad's response.

"Beautiful. So is this an invitation, or nah? – R. Martin."

Hmm.

Was it an invitation? It hadn't even been a full twenty-four hours since he left my apartment after running into Lauren. Was that too much?

A steady throb started between my thighs at the thought of having him there again, and I typed out *yes* in the reply box, but didn't hit send.

This *was* too much.

Throwing caution to the wind, going all in, having fun… that was exactly how I ended up addicted to Drew. I would never, *ever* do that again. And though Rashad and Drew were definitely different people — Rashad was cooler, more laid-back, *nicer* than Drew had ever been — there were certain similarities I couldn't ignore. One being an ability to strip away all of my abilities for self-control and self-preservation.

Rashad was *too* attractive, *too* good in bed, *too damned likable.*

Too much for me to trust myself not to end up in a repeat situation.

I didn't respond to his text, but marked it as read so it wouldn't keep showing up in my notification bar. I washed off my lipstick and put on a tee shirt, then crawled into bed, even though it wasn't even eight at night yet. It wasn't fair to *not* respond, and I knew that, but I couldn't think about what was fair for him... Rashad was grown. He would be fine. I had to worry about making sure *I* would be okay.

I almost dozed off, binge watching a series on Netflix when my phone chimed, making me flinch. I yawned, then picked it up, hoping it wasn't gonna be Rashad, wondering why I hadn't texted him back.

It wasn't Rashad.

I *wished* it was Rashad.

I would have absolutely rather put myself out there explaining my position to Rashad than replying to an email from someone I didn't want to talk to almost as much as I didn't want to talk to Drew.

His *mother*.

From: *FMRandle@ccjmail.com* *To:* *biancabadass@ccjmail.com*

Hi Bianca, it's Mama, she started, as if her maternal instinct had ever *really* applied to anyone other than her precious, infallible son. *I know it's been a while since we've spoken, but I wanted to reach out to you and see if you could find some time to speak with Drew.* My eyebrow hiked up almost to my scalp. Was this lady *serious*? *He says that you're ignoring him, and he doesn't know why because he's done nothing wrong. I know it probably seems a little unorthodox, for an almost thirty-year-old man's mother to reach out on his behalf, but I was hoping that woman to woman I'd be able to reach you. You and Drew have had so many ups and downs, and he's forgiven you for so much, honestly against my advice. After abandoning him for that silly dream of a website, I really do think the least you can do is have a conversation with my son when he's hurting. For whatever reason, he's still not over you after two years, and at this point I have to believe that you're stringing him along. Please stop this emotional warfare Bianca. I've considered you family since Drew brought you into my home, so mother to daughter, please make this right so everyone can move on.*

—Franchesca Randle

I sat there with my lips parted for a long time after I finished that message, because... *seriously?!* What... the... hell? Drew, forgave *me* for something? Me, stringing him along? Him, having done nothing wrong? Lavish on the Low, a *silly dream?* *Me* waging the emotional warfare?

"Okay, so screw his whole family," I mumbled under my breath as I blocked her too. She'd *never* been able to see her son as anything but a victim, in *anything*, so it didn't really surprise me that she'd view our relationship that way as well. What *did* surprise me was that it had taken so long. The last time she'd reached out had been a year ago, with a much more diplomatic message than this, asking me to "reconsider throwing our relationship away over a simple

miscommunication." I wondered what the heck he was telling her that she had it *so* twisted, but honestly... he could tell her every ugly detail of the truth, and she would still find a way to absolve him.

I stared at the *this user is now blocked* message plastered across my screen for a long moment, then navigated to the internet browser and typed *Drew Randle* in the search bar. My eyes went wide when I saw how... *not Drew* he looked in the most recent pictures that popped up. His deep mahogany skin seemed lackluster, his cheeks were starting to hollow from lost weight, his eyes were... *dead.* And then my gaze landed on a word that made my heart race.

Rehab.

Bad Boy Photographer Drew Randle Ordered to Rehab by Judge After Arrest for Disorderly Conduct in Hollywood Hotspot.

I closed the browser before I made myself sick. I hated him for what our relationship had done to me, but seeing him looking so tortured, so... uncared for... I couldn't stand that. It was so much easier to hate him when he was obviously healthy, and having his version of fun, and being an asshole, out loud. Arrested? Rehab? I couldn't find any joy in that.

Was he doing this because of me? If I talked to him, would it help? Would he stop— *no.* I plugged my phone into my charger and turned out the light, turning my focus back on the TV until I zoned out. I could not — *would not* — let Drew's drama take me to an ugly place... one where I really was thinking about calling him.

»——«

"Dammit, Rashad! Can you be serious for a whole two minutes, so we can get this done? My God." I rolled my eyes hard, then turned away from him as his face turned into a confused scowl.

It was mid-afternoon, and we were in the mostly-empty little gem of a consignment shop I'd found on the outskirts of the city. The lone worker was way up front, watching daytime soaps on a little TV beside the register, so Rashad and I pretty much had the place to ourselves.

I could understand his confusion, because really... he wasn't doing anything wrong — or at least outside of his normal character. He'd simply picked up one of those windbreaker outfits, with the zip-up jacket and matching pants from the rack, held it up, and made a joke about it. That was *all* I needed as an excuse to be a bitch to him, because I *needed* to be a bitch to him. What had previously been so easy for me was suddenly very, very hard.

It was nothing to be mean to him when he was saying or doing something that got on my nerves, but now... God help me, because my heart had started racing a little when I saw him in front of the shop, and he gave me that single dimpled smile. And when he pulled me into a greeting hug, the warmth of his body made me want to curl into a ball and stay close, the clean aroma of his cologne made me want to inhale deep. And the brief, private kiss he'd delivered near my ear, where no one else could see, but I definitely *felt*, made we wanna do... intimate things.

Further evidence that I *couldn't* handle a fling.

At least, not *this* type.

Rashad certainly wasn't the first person I'd slept with since Drew, but he *was* the first I'd slept with more than once. I wasn't trying to cuddle up and get close, make the night seem like anything it wasn't, and honestly... I wasn't impressed. Not that sex with Drew had been anything more than perfunctory in a *long* time by the time we broke up, but that was kind of the *point* of post-breakup sex. Someone who could do it better, make you forget about what you had, someone who could show you what you were missing.

Rashad *did* that, absolutely. He showed me, in action, the kind of sex I'd only read about, the care I'd only ever wished for, gave the kind of orgasms I'd only fantasized about. The *problem* though... the huge, catastrophic dilemma was that... sex wasn't the *only* area he was giving me things I was missing.

"Hey, what's up with you today?" Rashad gently grabbed my arm, turning off the camera around his neck. I'd complained about *that* too, that he wasn't even using a "real" video camera, but he said his Canon would give an excellent, clear video, while retaining a laid-back, casually filmed quality.

His ass thinks he knows everything.

"Bianca?"

I pulled myself away from my thoughts to glare at him, pulling my arm out of his grasp. "What?" I snapped.

"I asked you what was up with you? Why are you being all… anti-Rashad today? It's like everything I do is pissing you off."

I folded my arms over my chest. "So *you* piss me off, and the first question you ask is what's wrong with *me*, instead of looking at yourself? Really cute, Rashad. Typical, but—"

"O –*kay*. I see what's happening here," he interrupted. He glanced around us, and before I could ask what he was doing, he'd dragged me into an empty dressing room and locked the door behind us. He took off his camera and placed it on the bench seat, then approached me, backing me against the wall. "*Lips*, B."

"No." My answer was immediate, decisive, and short enough that my trembling voice wouldn't give away how much *both* of those words affected me. After that little… talk, at my apartment, about his *new rules*, I doubt Rashad could say the word *lips* around me without moisture pooling between my thighs. And something about *him* calling me "B" just… made me feel warm inside. It wasn't even like no one else called me that, it was actually pretty common, but out of *his* mouth… *damn.*

Rashad dipped his head so that we were at eye level. "Bianca… you can *give* them to me, or I'm gonna take 'em. I'm getting them either way."

"You realize that's a crime? And there's a *word* for that, Rashad, it's—"

"*Really*?" He shook his head in disbelief. "You're going

there, B, when you know I'm playing with you? What did I do between yesterday and today that has you acting like *this* with me again? I know we aren't the best of friends, but I thought we were past *this* shit."

I... couldn't answer that question. Because he *hadn't* done anything. It wasn't *him* at all, it was me. I turned my head away from him as my eyes watered, but he grabbed my chin, turning me right back to face him. Those dark golden-browns of his were filled with concern... *real concern*... and *that* made my eyes well with tears even faster, because when had any man besides the ones in my family *really* cared what was going on with me?

I gave a half-hearted attempt to push Rashad away from me, but he ignored it, instead enveloping me in his arms and picking me up to pull me close. Closing my eyes, I did what I'd wanted to do before and breathed him in as I buried my face in his neck, and relaxed my body into his.

"Hey... are you good?" he asked, squeezing me tight before he pulled back to see my face. "Why are you getting misty on me?" Shaking my head, I tried to tuck my head against his shoulder again, but he drew away. "Seriously, B. What's going on with you?"

"Nothing."

"It's *not* nothing."

"It *is*," I insisted. "It's no—"

Rashad swallowed those words with a kiss, pressing my back against the wall as he probed the seam of my lips with his tongue. There was a moment — a *teeny tiny* one — where I considered resisting, but then he gave me another soft, but insistent nudge, and I opened up to him. But I was *already* open to him. Way too far, and way too fast, and I didn't even quite understand why, but… here we were.

"Why are you doing this?" I asked, when he finally pulled away to let me catch my breath. "Tell me why you're… *like this*, with me."

He bunched his eyebrows together in confusion. "What do you mean *like this*? Like *what*?"

"So…so… I don't *know*." I blew out a frustrated breath, then wiggled my way out of his arms. With my feet back on the ground, and wearing flats, I had to tilt my head back to look into his face, and it made me feel… vulnerable.

I tried to move around him to the door, but he blocked my path, grabbing my arms to keep me in front of him. "Hold up now. Tell me what I'm being accused of here."

"Nobody's accusing you of anything."

He sucked his teeth. "The hell you aren't. You come in here acting like you caught me kicking baby animals down the road, then you say this *why are you doing this* shit… sounds like you feel like I did something, so I wanna know what it is."

"It's nothi—"

"You are *such* a goddamned liar."

Narrowing my eyes, I snatched away from his arms. "You can kiss my ass, okay?"

"Already done that, remember?" He smirked at me then, pushing his hands into his pockets, and *hell yes*, I remembered. The feeling of his gentle nips to my butt cheeks, followed by soft kisses to soothe the sting would probably always be burned into my mind.

"You need to grow up," I said, shoving past him to the entrance of the tiny room.

Before I could touch the latch to get out, Rashad was right behind me, pushing my body against the door. "And *you* need an attitude adjustment." I couldn't help the moan that escaped my throat as he pressed himself against my back, and a moment later, his hands were under my sweater dress, and inside my leggings and panties. His lips made contact with the back of my neck, but he kept his hand right at my pubic bone, not dipping lower. "Do you want me to stop?" he asked, brushing his mouth against my ear. I pressed my forehead to the cool painted wood surface of the door, and… shook my head, following it up with a whispered *no*.

My knees nearly buckled at the first contact of his fingers with the sensitive flesh between my thighs. He wrapped his other arm around me, keeping me pulled close, feeling his hardness against me. "*Shh shhh shhh,*" he murmured into my ear. "Don't want the cashier to come looking, do we?" He released his hold on my waist to put his hand over my mouth, muffling my sounds of pleasure as he stroked me into an orgasm that took… *no* time.

When I finally stopped panting, he removed his hand. I turned to face him, and watched, mesmerized, as he put that hand to his mouth and licked *me* off his fingers. It was enough to make me wet all over again, and I reached up, cupping his face in my hands to pull him down into a kiss.

"B," he said, when I let him go, "I don't know what Drew did to you, but understand... I don't have any type of... ulterior motive, or end game, nothing like that. I... *like you*, that's it. Other than that... I don't know what I'm doing. I'm just *doing*. I've had girlfriends, I've done friends with benefits, I've done *call me when you need to fuck, but that's all*. But *this*... this dynamic we've got going on... I've never done this shit before."

I swallowed hard, focusing my gaze on the buttons of his shirt. "And what dynamic is that Rashad?"

"One where..." He trailed off, then took a step back, scrubbing a hand over his head. "One where we're supposed to be in this for sex, no strings attached, but you stay on my mind when I'm not around you. Where I feel like I don't know you, but I wanna figure you out. Where the sex is honestly amazing, but... I kinda think I might want more than that."

Immediately, I started shaking my head. "I can't—"

"And I'm not asking you too," he said, raising his hands in defense. "Whatever it is you were gonna say, I'm not *asking* you for anything, B. I'm not about to ask you to be my girl, or get down on one knee, or whatever over-the-top shit is probably in your head right now. I'm chilling. *We're chillin'*. I'm letting you know where my head is at, so that next time you find yourself wondering why I'm *like this* with you... you already *know* why. Aiight?" I blushed as he advanced on me again, grabbing me at the waist. He grinned as he lowered his mouth to mine. "You already know, don't you?"

I offered my lips freely for him to take, and he did, with a leisurely, sweet kiss that made my toes curl in my boots. After a moment, I pulled away, then realized something that made me slap his arm. "So you *knew* what I meant when I asked you why you were *like this*, and started an argument with me instead of answering the question?"

He shrugged. "I didn't start an argument, I was trying to get clarity before I made an *assumption*. But yeah... I knew what you meant. You kinda seem... surprised by shit that my dad taught me as basic decency."

"Yeah right," I scoffed. "Holding me while I cry is basic?"

"When you're letting me in your bed, inside your body, yeah. It *is*."

His eyes and expression gave me sincerity, but... the sense of *too good for this not to be some shit that will make me look like a fool* kicked in, and I narrowed my eyes. "And what about those other girls, huh? When we first met, it was because you were *complaining*, about women who wanted more from you than sex. Did you hold them too, after you hurt their feelings, told them it would never be anything more for you?"

Rashad gave his head a slight tip to the side, then shook it as he chuckled dryly. "This is different, Bianca, and you know it."

"How so?" I crossed my arms.

"Because *you're* different," he countered, meeting the challenge in my eyes. "And how I feel about you is different. There probably *are* women who would call me every name in the book because they wanted something I wasn't willing to give, but they can't *ever* say I lied about that. They can't say I deceived them, can't say I was anything but a gentleman, can't say I treated them insensitively. If they *did* say that, it would be a lie, cause that's not how I was raised. So... If you want me to leave you alone, say it, but you'll have to find something else to throw in my face if you're trying to get me offended, or on the defensive. *That* ain't it."

I bit the inside of my cheek. "But I've told you to leave me alone before, and you didn't listen."

"I *did* listen, liar." He chuckled at my expression, then continued. "If *I* remember correctly, you told me to leave you alone, and then a week later you showed up at *my* apartment to seduce me."

"*Seduce* you?" I asked, propping my hands on my hips.

"What else would you call your fine ass showing up at a man's place at that time of night?"

"*Work*. Even though every time we *work* together, your fingers end up in me."

"*I'm tryna put something else in you*," Rashad said, cupping my face in his hands. "I'm ready for lips."

"You've *had* lips, multiple times today."

"And *now* I'm ready for the other ones."

"Rashad *stop*," I said, giggling as he tugged at the waistband to my leggings. "I'm *not* about to have sex with you in a dressing room."

He pushed me against the wall, gripping handfuls of my

ass as he pressed his body against mine. "So you can get *yours*, but I can't get mine?"

"It's *different*." I whimpered as he pressed his lips to my neck.

"How so?"

I met his eyes, with a wicked little grin. "Cause *I* can be quiet. You can't."

His eyes widened in amusement. "Is that right?"

"Mmmhmm."

I yelped as he smacked my ass, then moved back so we could get out of the door. "Come on. Let's hurry up with this so we can see about *that*."

With a smile that accepted his dare, I turned away, and had already stepped out of the dressing room when he grabbed my hand. "Hey," he said, pulling me close. "Seriously though... are you okay?"

I thought about that, but only for a brief moment. "Yeah... I am now." I tugged my hand away from his and went to the bathroom to fix myself up. In the mirror, I closed my eyes, thinking about the last fifteen minutes. But... I didn't know *what to think* about the last fifteen minutes. Rashad's parents had instilled decency, respect, and goodness in him. Drew's mother... gave him entitlement. Everything was about *him*, so it was no wonder that yeah... although I longed for the kind of attentiveness I got from Rashad, it made me suspicious.

And that was a damned shame.

I'd finally been able to see Drew for who he really was,

and recognized his toxic effect on me: It was hard to trust positive qualities in anyone else.

Rashad was waiting for me outside the bathroom, and we headed back out to the racks, where the cashier was still absorbed in the TV, and probably hadn't even noticed we'd left. I nodded to Rashad, and he raised the camera.

"Okay, Bianca Bailey. Tell everybody what we're doing here with this old raggedy stuff."

"It's *not* raggedy!" I insisted, shaking my head. "I know a lot of people think that, but you have to have a discerning eye, and you really can find gems."

"Like this?" Still holding up the camera, he picked up a huge faux fur hat from the top of one of the racks and put it on his head. "This shit is *hot*, right? What does it remind you of?"

He turned the camera to face himself for a shot, then made a face at the lens before he turned it back to face me.

"It's definitely... *something*," I said, leading him to the front door, which is where I wanted to start. "It makes you look like Jerome," I giggled. "A *playa from the Himalayaaas.*"

"Ahhh, *shit*, look at you, making jokes, okay, I see you," Rashad laughed, as he tossed the hat back onto the rack, then steadied the camera on me. "You ready to get started for real?"

"Yes. I am. Let's do it."

So... we did. And then... we went back to his place to *work* a little more.

»——«

"Let's talk *collaboration*."

I gave Cameron Taylor my undivided attention as she breezed into the room, upbeat as always, but looking a little less... *polished* than usual. I was almost certain it had a lot to do with tall, dark brown, and *sexy as hell* I'd seen palming her ass as he pulled her into her office and closed the door about fifteen minutes before this meeting.

Almost two weeks had passed since our first blogger segments went live on the magazine website, and we'd each done one more since then. They'd been well received enough to get Cameron ready to move forward with another idea, related to what she'd pitched in that very first meeting that brought us all together.

"In front of you," she said, gesturing to the table, "Are packets, customized for each of you. You've been assigned a partner, who is in a field that may be different from yours, but compliments your chosen genre well. Your packet includes ideas you can use, lists of resources, etc, everything you need to be successful in this endeavor, as long as you can work well with your partner. We want to film a few joint segments, rotating partners, and we'll see how it works out. You can open your packets!"

I hesitated with mine. I knew before my fingers even touched the seal that my partner was going to be Kieran. I *felt* it. And sure enough, when I *did* open it, there was his name paired with mine, staring at me.

He waved to me from the other end of the table, wearing a big smile across his handsome face, and I waved back, plastering on a smile of my own. It wasn't that there was anything *wrong* with Kieran... not exactly, I just wasn't so sure of working with him. I still got that *fetish* feeling from him, even though his flirtation seemed genuine, and he was honestly sweet.

"How ya' doin', partner?" he asked, putting on a false country twang as he approached me after the meeting, with his thumbs tucked into the loops of his belt.

Shaking my head, I pretended to tip a hat to him. "I'm doing good, Kieran. You?"

"Much better now that I know I'm gonna have a *gorgeous* partner for this project." He shot me one of his bright, winning smiles, and I blushed because I couldn't help it.

"Yeah right," I teased. "I bet you wish you'd gotten Raisa or Asha."

"Not a chance," he shot back. "I got *exactly* who I wanted." Kieran stepped a little closer to me, wrapping me in the scent of his cologne, and the smile he gave me then was... different. It wasn't innocent, or charming... it was *intentionally* sexy. "So... we should probably make some time to get together, decide what we're gonna do?"

"Umm... yeah." I took a subtle half-step backward. "We probably should."

"Let's start with dinner then. Tonight. I can pick you up at seven."

My eyes widened at the boldness of him setting a time

for dinner before I'd even agreed, but I simply laughed, then said, "How about I *meet* you at seven?"

"Sounds like a date." He shot me one last smile, and before I could correct *that* notion, he was gone, seeking out Cameron for something, and Raisa had sidled up to me.

"That looked *cozy*," she said, grinning as she looped her arm in mine, just like always.

This time, I just returned her smile. "*Why* does this feel like déjà vu?"

Raisa put a finger to her chin, and tilted her head. "Hmm... maybe because I *always* come running over to see what's going on when I see Kieran grinning in your face. I'on like him," she said, turning up her nose as she glanced in his direction.

"Wait a minute," I laughed. "What happened to you making up that I was interested in sports to get me and him talking?"

She shrugged. "That was back when he was just fine, and I hadn't talked to him yet. *Now* I think his ass is... too well put-together or something. *Too*... supposedly sweet and innocent."

"Mmmhmm. Is that right?"

"Yes, it is. And it doesn't have *anything* to do with me wanting you to get with Rashad." She gave me a bright smile, and started to walk away, but I dragged her back, then pulled her into an empty corner of the room.

"*What* are you talking about, Raisa?" I asked, glancing over her shoulder to make sure no one was around.

Shaking her head, she leaned in my direction. "Girl I'm

not *blind*. I saw how cozy y'all were at my house the other night. Next time you wanna be sneaky, *don't* use my balcony. You guys were hidden from the living room, but from *my* room I could see your nasty asses damn near screwing on my outdoor furniture."

I blushed over *that*, remembering exactly the night she was talking about. Rashad had been away for some assignment all week, and against my better judgement... I missed him. Even though we'd texted at least a little bit every day.

Raisa had another get-together at her place, and I agreed to go, not knowing, but *hoping* that Rashad would be there too. I couldn't recall *ever* feeling as good with a man as I'd felt when he snuck up from behind as I passed the kitchen, pulling me into his arms. Even though it was chilly out, he'd taken me outside for privacy, and we stayed there, kissing and touching until a sudden clap of thunder and downpour of rain drove us inside.

"Girl, you should see the look on your face," she giggled, shaking her head. "You wanna tell me what's *really* going on with you and my brother?"

I shrugged, then sighed, tossing my head back against the wall as I considered her question. Finally, I brought my gaze back to hers, and said, "Nothing. We're... *friends*, I guess."

"*Friends?* Bianca... please. Even *I* know it's more than that. I'm not trying to intervene on his behalf or anything, but if it matters... he *really* likes you." She raised her hands. "Now, I know, *I know*, you're off the market. I actually warned Rashad about that a few weeks ago, to not end up getting his feelings hurt, but... B... it seems to me like you *really* like him too. I swear, I *swear* I'm not trying to meddle, but if you two like each other... don't let fear of another heartbreak be the thing that keeps you apart."

I'd confided in Raisa about Drew, which I didn't necessarily regret, but now that she knew the story... she *insisted* that I was giving him too much power in my life still. I spent ten minutes explaining to her that I wasn't interested in taking the risk again of being changed by love, like I had with Drew, only for her to brush it off.

"I don't think you're *really* afraid of being changed by love, Bianca," she'd responded, waving her hand like she was brushing away my words. "I think you're afraid of love letting you be *exactly* who you are. You're using this belief in love as a grand manipulator to justify not taking another risk. How long are you gonna live like that?"

I left that conversation pissed off at her, feeling like she wasn't even trying to understand. I'd gone from a bubbly, happy teenage girl with plenty of friends, to one who stayed at home waiting for a call or email from a man who wasn't even thinking about me, unless I was right in front of his face. And hell, sometimes I questioned *that* too. But I was *in love*. That was how it started. Another boy couldn't even look my way without me scrambling to get out of his view, so Drew wouldn't possibly get jealous. No short-shorts, no crop tops, plain earrings, hair kept long, styled simply, basic makeup, if any at all, because that was how *he* insisted it should be when I was *his* girl. I was *his*, so why did I need to make myself attractive to others... even myself?

I was several years older, and off in college when I realized the lapse in *that* logic, but I was still with him. Because I was *used* to him. He was my first boyfriend, my first love, my first *everything*. Like he said... I couldn't go off to college and *leave him*. That became a "thing" later too, whenever I got enough sense to threaten to break up with him. Drinking, getting in trouble, acting out because I'd "abandoned" him. Building up the sense of guilt that would later make me stay.

So I went to his alma mater. He'd already graduated, but he was around often, chasing other girls right in my face. It was funny though... the girls he gravitated to wore those short-shorts, had crazy fun hair, big hoop earrings, bright makeup... everything he discouraged in me.

But he loved me like I was, or so he said. I didn't *need all of that*, to be pretty. It *didn't look right on me* anyway, according to him. And as stupid as it was, I *loved him*...so I believed it. Every word that came out of his mouth, every insult, every criticism... I believed. Cause nobody was telling me any different. Lauren was too young to even catch what was going on, and my dad was still in the military then, and always on a plane. There was nobody to tell me what I knew now, that he was *grooming* me, into a doormat to use as he pleased.

And... it was working. It was working *well*, until I ran across a post from one of my favorite bloggers, talking about how she'd finally left an abusive relationship, after many, *many* years. I was lucky enough that Drew was never physically abusive with me, but the things she listed as emotional abuse resonated *strongly* with me. It still took a while before I *really* woke up... but she planted a seed.

Raisa put her hand over mine, interlacing our fingers, and the contact brought my thoughts back to our conversation. "I *know* Rashad, and he wouldn't do anything to hurt you... not like Drew did. And I'll personally kick his ass if he does," she laughed. "And to be fair, if you guys go for it, I'll kick *your* ass if you hurt *him*." She giggled at herself after that, but then her expression turned serious again. "I'm laughing... but I'm not kidding."

Shaking my head, I chuckled. "I know you're not kidding, Raisa. Thank you. I know you're looking out for your brother."

She patted my hand, then walked away with a smile, leaving me alone with my thoughts, which were now firmly centered on Drew, wondering what the hell I needed to do to *really* get myself over him.

A few moments later, my cell phone buzzed, notifying me of a new email message. I didn't recognize the address, but I opened it and read the message. Then... I read it again.

It was from Drew's rehabilitation counselor... requesting a meeting.

nine

. . .

bianca

I REALLY SHOULD HAVE KNOWN BETTER.

When it came to *anything* involving Drew, I should have known that there was some kind of catch, something I wasn't being told, some *gotcha* that wasn't immediately clear. Instead, I got that heart-rending email from Drew's addiction counselor, talking about how he needed some type of resolution to our relationship to continue moving forward, and I hopped my ass on the first plane there.

My thought going in was that this was my chance to finally, officially end this chapter, to get some closure, since Drew refused to hear me. In the presence of his counselor, he couldn't tell me I was being dramatic, couldn't "give me some time to cool off", couldn't talk me into believing that *no one else wanted me anyway, so quit playin'.* Being nice hadn't worked, being mean hadn't worked, and ignoring him wasn't working either. So maybe *this* would.

I didn't tell anybody I was going. This was *my* battle to fight, my journey to complete… there was no reason to involve anyone else, especially when I knew my dad, Lauren, and even Raisa would have tried to talk me out of it. And Rashad… I still wasn't ready to give in to *that* level of emotional intimacy with him. What we had going on now was perfect. No bullshit about *what we were to each other*, or *where we saw this going*. No pressure, no stress, just hot sex, texting marathons, late night phone calls about random topics, and booty rubs in the dark.

Perfect.

This mess with Drew went beyond that, though. It involved digging into baggage that was best for me to sort through on my own, so I walked into Pathways Rehab Center alone, with my head held high, intending to do that.

My first impression of the center was that it looked more like a luxury resort than what I expected from a treatment facility, but… it *was* Drew. He had money, his parents had money… of course he'd come to a world-class place.

At the reception desk, a skinny brunette confiscated my phone, *"to preserve the confidentiality and privacy of all visitors"*, then led me through the polished marble halls to a set of doors. Through those doors was a private seating area, featuring live greenery and waterfalls. At the end of *that*, there was another set of doors. I followed her through those to yet *another* door, which she gestured me through with a plastered-on smile.

The first place my gaze landed was on Drew, and he looked a *lot* better than those googled pictures… more like the Drew I knew before. He was thinner than usual, but still handsome, with smooth dark skin and chiseled features. I wasn't used to the thick layer of hair covering his jaw and chin, but it was nice on him. Made him look more distinguished.

Unfortunately, that was the only positive moment of nostalgia, because as soon as our eyes met, I felt... paralyzed. A slow, satisfied smile crept across his face, and that was the moment, *right there*, where I knew that coming here was going to rank pretty high on the stupidest mistakes of my life.

"You must be Bianca." I tore my eyes away from Drew to see a tall, handsome man with perfectly coiffed blonde hair. I assumed the Ken doll to be the counselor, and that was confirmed when he reached to shake my hand, introducing himself as Dr. Scott.

Anxiety prickled my skin as I sat in the chair he indicated as mine, and I noticed then that there was a fourth person in the room.

Francesca Randle.

"Good to see that you *do* still understand basic communication skills Bianca. I was beginning to think you couldn't read or speak, since you've not responded to any of our attempts at correspondence," she said, folding her hands in her lap as she stared at me.

I ran my tongue over my lips, and after a heavy sigh, said, "I have *no* interest in arguing with, or even engaging with you, Ms. Randle. I'm here strictly to resolve things between Drew and me. I'm not going to sit here and be insulted."

"And we don't expect you to," Dr. Scott chimed in. "Mrs. Randle is here to serve as support for her son, who is in a fragile state. The focus of this session is you and Drew."

I shot Mrs. Randle a last look of disgust before I turned away, focusing my gaze on the only person who didn't make me want to vomit — Dr. Scott.

"So let's go ahead and get started, shall we?" he asked, sitting forward. "Drew… why don't you tell me how seeing Bianca here today makes you feel?"

Keeping my eyes downward, I forced myself not to tremble as Drew's gaze raked over me, ravaging me until he stopped on my breasts. "It makes me feel happy, that she finally stopped ignoring me. I'm glad that she cared enough to come today. I'm… disappointed, in what she's done to her face, and hair, and body."

I rolled my eyes, biting my lip to keep from telling him exactly where he could shove his disappointment… and his happiness for that matter.

"What about you Bianca?" Dr. Scott smiled as I looked up. "How does seeing Drew make you feel?"

I smirked at first, then shook my head. "None of you want to hear that answer."

"Actually we do," the counselor nodded. "This is a safe space, Bianca. You can say what you feel."

With a scoff, I sat back in my chair, looking over Drew's shoulder to the ocean view from the window. "I feel… anxious. I *don't* feel safe. I feel like I'm back in a place I don't wanna be... in a cage." I regretted revealing that information almost as soon as the words crossed my lips, because I could swear I saw smug satisfaction in Drew's eyes when I chanced a look directly into his face. "I think I made a mistake, in coming here. I'm going to g—"

"Wait a minute," Drew interrupted, raising a hand. "Let's figure this out, put it all on the table. What is this *about*, Bianca? We took a break, and now it's time to stop playing. If it's about your little blog or whatever, fine, you can keep that. And we can talk about the hair and the piercings. It's unattractive, and you can't be my girl walking around looking like that. I guess you don't know better, but this is why you should have listened to me. I was trying to help you."

I narrowed my eyes, lips parted as I waited for him to laugh, smile, anything to indicate that he was joking. When it never came, I ran my tongue over my teeth in disgust. "Do you even *hear* yourself? I run a *huge* fashion and beauty blog, but you really think you can tell me what is and isn't attractive? *Newsflash*, any adjustments I make to my appearance aren't *for you*, or the *next* man, or *anybody else*. My hair is purple because *I* think it's cute, and I'm considering red and green for the holidays, and I'm feeling downright friggin' *festive*, how about *that*? I have tattoos because *I* like them, piercings because *I* like them, and I couldn't give *less* of a damn about whether or not it's attractive to you *or* your mama. You can't control me, can't hurt me. My life *was* about you— not anymore."

"This is the dramatics I referred to, Dr. Scott." Mrs.

Randle shook her head at me, then turned back to the counselor. "You see how she acts as if my Drew is some monster, who brutalized her? He's been nothing except kind to her, even as a teenager, when I warned him about little fast-tailed girls like her. But he *insisted*, so I welcomed this… little… *harlot*, into our lives, into my home. I knew she was motherless, so I had to tell Drew how to handle her, how to *mold* her into—"

"*Mold* me?" I interrupted, my eyebrows drawn together in a frown. "Mold me *how*?"

Again, Mrs. Randle shook her head. "I recognized you for what you were as soon as I saw you, because I used to be the same thing. Drew's father had to teach me too, but *I* was willing to learn how to be a proper lady, instead of a strong willed, purple haired, pierced—"

"Okay *screw you*. I'm not doing this," I snapped, pulling myself up from my chair. "I don't know what kind of psycho-cult bullshit you called yourself pulling me into, but I'm so glad I got the hell away from you and your son when I did."

"Damnit, Bianca." Against my will, I froze at the sound of Drew's voice. I could feel the shift in energy as he approached me, sending a fresh wave of cold anxiety rushing through my chest. "I thought we were going to try to work this out? I'm sitting in rehab, and you're still gonna abandon me?"

Those words snapped the paralysis out of me. "*Abandon* you?" I asked sharply, turning to face him. "Are you *kidding*? You know… most of that time we were together, you had me thinking *I* was crazy, like *I* was the problem. But it's not *me*! You people are *insane,* and I don't know what kind of "treatment center" this is, but Drew I really hope you go somewhere to get you some *real* help." I glanced at "doctor" Scott and threw my hands in the air. "Is this *really* what you people do here? Call *victims* in to be berated and attacked, so your patients can feel better? This isn't *helping* him!"

"The only *help* my son needs is to be rid of *you*." Mrs. Randle shot those words out like I should be offended, but instead, I turned to her and gave her a few quick handclaps.

"*Bravo,*" I said, leaning in her direction. "The first sensible thing that has come out of anybody's mouth. *Please* get over me. *Please* forget I existed. *Please* lose my number. Tell me what I can do to facilitate this, *please*."

"Now Bianca, let's calm down." Dr. Scott put a hand on my shoulder, exerting gentle pressure to direct me back into my seat, but I snatched away.

"I will *not* calm down. I'm getting the hell out of here. I hope you all have a *terrible* day." I tried to get around Dr. Scott, but he gripped me at the arms, holding me still.

"This is a healing place. We don't speak to each other that way around here. We're going to sit down, calm down, and figure out what we need to do to move the relationship forward. Your presence here indicates that you want the same thing."

I snatched away from him *again,* shoving him out of my space as I backed toward the door. "My *presence here* indicates that I'm trying to move *past* this relationship, *not* forward. I came here for *closure!* I haven't spoken to Drew in *two years*, and you thought I wanted to get back together?"

"So you're really doing this?" Drew asked, stepping forward again. "*Seriously?* We were together for damned near seven good years, Bianca. And now… nothing?"

I shook my head, throwing my hands up in the air. "*Good* years, Drew? I spent my teenage years toning myself down, trying to compete with college girls for your attention. I spent my college years competing with my own peers, plus grown ass women, for *your* attention, again. When I was supposed to *have it*, because you said you *loved* me. Everything you said, I believed. Everything you told me would make you happy, I did. Because it was *you*," I said, my voice breaking with emotion as tears sprang to my eyes. "But you know… that's not your fault. You did what you did, screwing any and every body you wanted, leaving me waiting for you, dragging my confidence through the mud, convincing me that I wasn't worthy of anybody or anything else because I *let* you. And that's *my* bad. But what I *won't* ever do again, is *that*. You, nor anybody else can have control of me. You didn't kill my spirit then, and you're not about to do it now. I'm leaving," I said with force to Dr. Scott, daring him to block me again. This time, he stepped aside, and I stomped to the door, unmoved by the heavy silence in the room.

Just before I opened the door, I turned back, looking Drew right in the face. "Do *not* call me. Do *not* email me. *Do not contact me in any way.* You, your mother, your cousins, whoever. I *hoped* you would go away, but since I have to say this explicitly, *again*: Leave me the hell alone, or I have no problem involving the authorities. Which is what I should have done in the first place, but I wanted to ignore the problem. I thought you would get it, but you don't, so... here we are. *Leave me alone.* Okay?"

I flung the door open then stepped out, and I started to slam it behind me, but then I thought of something else and stuck my head back in the room. "Oh, and by the way, if I'm *so* unappealing, such a damned hassle, have so much to learn... why do you want me? Huh? So you can have someone to "mold"? Screw that. And so you know, you are *so far* from the only person who *wants* me that it's hilarious. The purple hair and tats and piercings haven't stopped a single soul from stepping to me... including your *homeboy* Rashad. Meditate on *that*, asshole."

Then, I *did* slam the door behind me. I stomped through the halls of that place back to the front, snatched my cell phone when the receptionist gave it back, and barged out of the front door. I didn't stop until I was closed in my rental car, and I only gave myself a moment to catch my breath even then. Not until I was off the *Pathways* property, had purchased a *new* airline ticket, and was safely in my seat on the plane did I feel some measure of peace again. Tears burned the inside of my eyelids, but I willed myself not to let them free, not *here*.

When I was finally home, they came. Hot, fat, uncontrollable tears that took my breath away, the kind of cry that I'd... *never* had. Yeah, some of those tears were because it hurt that someone I gave my heart and body to for seven years *still* thought very, *very* little of me. But… more than that, I felt… strangely *free*. I'd stood in front of him and his *stupid ass mama* without being broken again. I'd said what I needed, stood up for myself, showed him, unequivocally, that *he did not own me*. He didn't control me.

I really was free.

From my curled up position in my bed, buried under the covers, I heard a knock at my front door. I drug myself from my warm cocoon and went to the door, looking through the peephole. With a heavy sigh, I bumped my head gently against the door, pressing my hand to the surface.

"I can hear you on the other side of the door," Rashad called out, the sound of his voice making my heart clench. "I know, I know, it's late, and I didn't call or anything, but… you've been kinda out of pocket for the last couple of days. I… wanted to see your face, make sure you were good. And I've got pad thai, which I know you love, so… open the door, B."

I closed my eyes as a fresh round of tears sprang forth.

"If you've got wack-ass Kieran in there, I'm kicking his wack ass."

I burst out laughing at that, and then… without even bothering to dry my face, I unlocked the door and flung it open. Neither of us said anything. I stood there, waiting for his response to my current state, but he simply… stared. In my head, I willed him to say something, but instead, his expression softened and he stepped in, pushing me further into the apartment.

He closed and locked the door behind him, then placed a large, fragrant bag of food on the table beside it before turning back to me. A moment later, I was in his arms, and... the dam of tears broke again. Still, Rashad said nothing, just rocked me back and forth, rubbing my back until my sobs finally stopped, and I moved to pull away.

"Do you wanna talk about... whatever this is?" he asked, using his thumbs to wipe my face.

I shook my head, quickly. "*No*. Not... not now. I just... can we...?" I looked him in the eyes as I lowered my hands to his belt, fingering the buckle.

He cocked an eyebrow. "I mean... if that's what you wanna do, I'm down, but... you sure? We don't *have* to do that. I didn't come over here for *that*. We can—"

"Shut up," I said, looping my arms around his waist as I rested my head against his chest. "Before you make me cry again."

Rashad chuckled, then put his arms around me too, resting his hands on my ass. "Did I do something wrong?"

"Uh-uh," I mumbled into his shirt, nuzzling my face in the soft fabric before I looked up to meet his gaze. "Not at all."

ten

· · ·

rashad

I DIDN'T UNDERSTAND what this girl was doing to me.

I mean… I understood it, I just didn't like it.

Well… it's not that I don't like it, but… *goddamn it.*

Bianca had my head all messed up.

I didn't wanna make it seem like whatever was happening between us was more than it was, but it was definitely, *definitely* more than we pretended, and more than either of us intended it to be.

Watching her move around her tiny kitchen, with her face emanating a peacefulness I'd *never* seen… my father's warning played in my head. *The kind of trouble you want to avoid, but can't. A woman who catches you off guard, and makes your brain go a little bit haywire, who you can't keep off your mind no matter how hard you try.* Yeah… that was definitely B.

Part of me felt like it was… too soon to be wrapped up

in this one girl, like I was too young to be wondering if she might be… yeah. Way too soon for that.

We were chillin'.

I should chill. That thought resonated, and held, but it didn't keep me from thinking about how easy it would be to get used to this half-naked breakfast thing we had going on right now. Sure, we'd only known each other a month, and only been sleeping together a few weeks, but I wouldn't exactly *hate* waking up with Bianca in my arms. It wouldn't be *so* bad to brush our teeth next to each other all the time like we had that morning, or made an effortless decision to work together on breakfast, as if we did it all the time.

I knew I was out of my mind to even be thinking about all of that, but… still.

Bianca glanced up at me with a smile as she turned to drop a handful of eggshells in the trash, then went to wash her hands. Her mood was markedly different from the night before, when she'd cried in my arms about unknown burdens, then fell asleep in my lap on her couch. She seemed… *lighter*, somehow. *Happier.*

"I thought you said you were helping. You're not gonna get breakfast if you're gonna sit there and watch, Shad," she said, coming to stand near my seat at her counter, with her hand propped on her hip. Her pretty brown skin was scrubbed clean of any makeup, her hair was all over the place, and she was…

"You're fucking *gorgeous.*"

Her eyes widened a little, lips parted before she

dropped her gaze as she blushed. Looking up again, she shook her head. "Flattery won't get food on these plates any faster."

"Can I have *you* on a plate instead?" I grabbed her waist, hauling her against me to bury my face in her neck, and kiss her there. She giggled, squirmed, but didn't move away, letting out a sigh bordering dangerously on *contentment* as I pulled her up, and into my lap. With one hand cupping my chin, she used the other to gently stroke my face, letting her fingertips linger over my dimple. "You keep touching me like this, I'm gonna fall asleep."

"Let's do it," she said, resting her head on my shoulder. "Breakfast can wait... I'm honestly still drained anyway."

"From what?"

Bianca stiffened in my arms immediately at that question, then sat up, apprehension filling her eyes as she met my gaze. After a heavy sigh, she said, "So maybe breakfast *can't* wait. We... We can talk after that."

Saying nothing else, she got up from my lap and went back to the counter on the other side of the kitchen, where she resumed whisking the eggs she'd cracked into a glass bowl. My gaze traveled up the backs of her bare thighs, to where her butt cheeks peeked from the bottom of her boyshort panties. That sight made me go to her, wrapping my arms around her waist to pull her against me. The whisk dropped from her fingers as I kissed her neck.

"These eggs are never gonna get on this stove if you don't stop."

"So?" I asked, pulling her earlobe between my teeth. "Fuck those eggs, girl."

"*Shad...*"

I groaned, tightening my grip as I rocked against her, letting her feel *exactly* what she did to me. "You sure? This counter is the perfect height... I could bend you over... hell, you could keep stirring if you wante—"

"Rashad Martin!" Bianca scolded, wiggling to turn around and face me. Her voice was harsh, but her eyes danced with amusement. "*After* breakfast... but before we talk... okay?"

I jokingly poked out my lip, but agreed. I helped her finish our breakfast of bacon, eggs, and half a carton of fresh strawberries from her fridge. We cleaned the kitchen together, and afterwards she grabbed my hand to lead me back to her bedroom, but I picked her up, pressing her to the wall in the hallway instead.

She looped her legs around my waist, arms around my neck, eagerly accepting my tongue as I pushed it into her mouth. I wanted Bianca *bad*, always did, but something about this morning was different. Something, somewhere had shifted or was about to, and it wasn't necessarily bad, just... *different.*

I pushed her panties to the side and slipped a first, then second finger into her, groaning as her warmth surrounded me. She was already wet, and ready. She'd *been* wet and ready since last night, which I knew even though I hadn't touched her sexually at all. I *felt* it. It was one more thing in a growing list of ways that Bianca and I *vibed* together. Like last night, when I'd stopped to pick up dinner, and had the sudden urge to order enough for two, when I hadn't even spoken to her. Or last week, when I was leaving mine and Raisa's new workspace, and swung by the Sugar&Spice offices after hours "just because" and found Bianca doing test runs for her next video in the studio space.

If somebody asked why *her*... I couldn't answer that question. Cause I didn't know *why Bianca*, other than to acknowledge that there was this *feeling*, that this, whatever we were doing... this was *real*. This wasn't *just* sex, we weren't *just* friends, this wasn't *just* a fling. This wasn't the same kind of playing I'd done in the past, and this wasn't even the same as the few occasions I'd "caught feelings" before, only to have the relationships fizzle out. It was different because *Bianca* was different, and complex, and passionate, and... beautiful. Bianca was absolutely trouble, but she was *right*.

Every little whimper, every moan, every gasp of pleasure that escaped her mouth made me want her more, but I forced myself to be patient, to take my time. I plunged deeper, circled my thumb faster, reveled in the feeling of her body clenching around my fingers. Leaning forward, I captured her mouth again with mine, sucking the lingering flavor of our breakfast fruit from her lips. She pressed the back of her head to the wall, watching me through half-lidded eyes, mouth open as she panted for breath.

Our eyes met, and she bit her lip, and then as we looked at each other, my hand still moving between her legs, *there it was again*, more shifting, more of... whatever was making this *different*. She moved her hands from my shoulders, and the next place I felt them was the waistband of my boxers, tugging it down, and then her fingers were around my erection, and she was pushing *my* fingers away.

I took her hint, and with a couple of quick movements I was inside of her, sinking deep as she dug her fingernails into my hips. I grinned as she involuntarily rolled her eyes upward, then closed them as I started moving. We maneuvered her shirt off, and I dipped my head to her chest, closing my mouth over one hardened nipple then the other as I moved us into the corner.

I unhooked one of her legs from my waist and pressed into the wall, opening her wider, using her ankle as an anchor as I plunged deeper. Her mouth was wide open, letting out breathless little cries and yelps of pleasure until her body erupted in satisfying jerks and quivers. Those breathless sounds gained volume and weight as she moaned my name in my ear, over and over, turning me on even more, making me harder as I delved deeper, until she came undone.

She held me tight, her body quaking in my grip as she clawed my back, making a sound somewhere between a scream and a purr. I growled right back at her as I came undone too, because *goddamn* she felt good, and I was … *lost* in the feeling of being inside her, all tight and warm and *so wet*.

Afterwards, we showered together, where we had each other again. By the time we actually made it to her bedroom, it was almost noon, and a nasty thunderstorm had rolled in. Even though it was the middle of the day, the sky was dark. We left the lights off anyway, laying naked on our backs across the bed, the sound of the rain serving as background music for… whatever was about to happen.

"I went to see Drew," she said, in a tone that was probably supposed to mask the emotion behind her words, but the fact that she felt the need to mask it said… everything.

I swallowed, keeping my gaze trailed on the ceiling. "So what happened?"

It took her such a long time to say anything that I wondered if she'd heard me. But then, she let out a little puff of breath. "Fuck Drew. That's what happened."

Bianca sat up, looking toward the partially opened blinds that covered the window. The line of her back, curve of her hips, soft mounds of her breasts, not small, but not exactly large, were outlined in the semi-darkness. She shifted again, looking down at her hands, and her thick, lush eyelashes rested against her cheeks, creating a scene in front of me that made me wish I had my camera.

"I was… *bubbly*," she said, glancing over at me. "Always in bright colors, and made up outfits from my auntie's closet, and always *talking*." She smiled, then shook her head. "Always friendly… and I *loved* boys, and they loved me. But I wasn't giving up any ass though," she giggled. "Nope. I didn't want a boyfriend, I liked flirting, and being Bianca. I was *happy*. And… then I met Drew, and I let him change me."

I listened without interruption as she gave me the

"highlight reel" of her and Drew's relationship. She closed herself in, pulling her knees up to her chest, wrapping her arms around her legs as she talked. The more she said, the angrier I got, and by the time she reached the end, which was telling me about her visit to him in rehab, I'd already made a decision: I was kicking ole boy's ass, on sight.

"Did he ever put his hands on you?" I wasn't even sure why I asked that question, because if the answer had been yes, I probably would have asked Bianca where that gun of hers was. Luckily for Drew — and my potential criminal record — she shook her head.

"No. He wasn't abusive. At least... not like that."

She smiled at me, but it was weak, and she looked so vulnerable for a second that it made those "allegations" of inappropriateness with teenage models come to mind. Everybody knew he'd done that shit, he just had enough money to pay people off, and turn truth to "rumors". And if he was offensive with *them*, I didn't even really want to think about what he may have inflicted on Bianca.

But I had to ask.

"B...," I started, reaching across the bed for her hand. She gave it, then laid down again, moving until she was snuggled up close to my side. "Did he ever... make you do anything you didn't wanna do?"

Her silence after that question spoke volumes, and *I* sat up then, fully intending to go *find* Drew, but she put a hand to my shoulder. "Rashad...I did a lot of things I didn't *want* to do with and for Drew. Because I wanted his love, I wanted his attention. And that's my fault. Nobody threatened to harm me, or my family. *Made me* is... it's a gray area, you know?"

"Stop making excuses for his punk-ass. You were naïve, okay, but I know for a fact *his ass* is... a fucking predator. Did he ever force himself on you?"

She frowned. "You mean... like...?"

"Did he ever act like you said *yes*, when you actually said *no*?"

She shook her head, drawing her legs up to her chest again. "I... never *said* no. He made it seem like... it was the biggest slight in the world if I said no, unless I was on my period. If I didn't say yes, he wouldn't speak to me for weeks. And... I was a teenager, you know? I lost my virginity to him, he was my first boyfriend, he was everything to me. So when he asked, I gave. And eventually he stopped *asking*, he just *took*, because it was always a yes anyway."

"Bianca... *why?*" I asked, trying not to be affected by the hitch in her voice, or the fact that her eyes had welled with tears. "You're smart, and vivacious, and beautiful... you didn't *have* to put up with that shit from him."

Shrugging, she stretched out her legs, wiggling her toes in front of her. "When you hear a story like mine, everybody expects me to say that there was some childhood trauma, or that I have daddy issues, or something like that, right? But... that's not the case. I was a sixteen year old girl, who got involved with a nineteen year old guy and lost herself. I wasn't a girl with no friends, longing for a companion, or... *anything* like that. Drew... and apparently his mother, knew what they were doing. I didn't. I got caught up."

"So your parents didn't have anything to say?"

"My parents didn't *know*. My mother died of cancer, when Lauren was three years old. I was nine. My father is — well, *was* — in the military. His field was training, so he was gone a *lot*. Lauren and I were basically raised by my mother's sister, and she wasn't exactly... attentive. I mean, she was there for whatever we needed, and we never lacked for anything... except maybe guidance and attention. But... in any case... that's my *past*. I'm over Drew, I'm looking forward. I had a wakeup call, and I have a *much* better grasp on who I am, what I'm worth. And recent events have made me... rethink a couple of my views on some things."

I lifted an eyebrow. "Things like what?"

"Things that I am *not* about to discuss with you," she said, giving me a big, *genuine* smile that lit up her whole face. "Maybe... much later. But not now. We'll see."

I grinned back, pulling her onto my lap. "We'll see, huh? When?"

"I already told you — *much later*. But... there is something you can do for me *right now*." She draped her arms over my shoulders, moving until our hips were pressed together, and we were chest to chest.

"Yeah? What's that?"

Bianca pressed her mouth to mine. "Gimme those lips, Shad."

»——«

Bianca.

»——«

"You know you're looking good enough to eat tonight, right?"

Rashad murmured those words in my ear and then stepped back, but I could feel his eyes on my ass, admiring how it looked in the dress I'd chosen for tonight's event. I'd known about Sugar&Spice's anniversary event for a while, and knew it was kind of a big deal, but with everything else going on, it hadn't been on my mind until Raisa asked me what I was wearing.

Limos, red carpet, celebrities, all that jazz... it really wasn't my type of party. I would honestly rather be with my family or friends, but again... this event was kind of a big deal. Because we were connected to Sugar&Spice, we had to dress in black, purple, or white, which were the magazine's colors. I chose white. It was simple, no bling, no cutouts or anything like that. Full length sleeves, and the neckline came up to my collar, so I wasn't showing any skin, but the way that slinky fabric clung to my curves, perfectly fitted to my body... I felt incredible. And if the look in Rashad's eye was any indication, I *looked* incredible too.

We didn't come to the event together, but he approached me as soon as I arrived, putting that naughty little compliment in my ear. He'd been gone again all week, and was showing his face for a few minutes before he had to leave, so I guess he figured he needed to get his in-person flirting in while he could. Not that I minded.

I'd beat myself up for that disastrous trip to visit Drew, but really... it was pretty damned liberating. Seeing him again, hearing him spout his ridiculous truths about me and our relationship made it even clearer that the problem was *him*, not me. And Rashad's presence afterward... that gave me hope.

It wasn't like I was *in love* with Rashad or anything, because it was *way, way* too soon for anything like that. But suddenly... I wasn't so repulsed by the idea of becoming emotionally invested in someone. Liking Rashad, and enjoying being around him... it no longer felt like a weakness. I couldn't pinpoint when it happened, couldn't identify the exact moment when things shifted, but there was this *feeling* whenever I was around him. Almost like a tap on my shoulder, and a whisper in my ear, that hey... *this* is a guy you can trust with your heart.

Still though... I knew I needed to be cautious. Even though Rashad gave me butterflies, and made me laugh, and made me feel... *safe*... I couldn't be the same Bianca that got caught up in a man and lost who she was. Not ever, *ever* again. But that didn't mean I couldn't enjoy what we were doing now.

I still had a big smile on my face from Rashad's comment as I stepped onto the red carpet area where the Sugar&Spice logo background was, with him close behind. It wasn't until cameras started flashing in my face that I wiped the goofy grin from my expression, remembering that this was a large, widely covered event.

I wasn't necessarily a celebrity, but people were serious about their online personalities, and in *that* realm, especially for a black girl in the genre... *I* was kind of a big deal, even though I didn't like to think about it that way. The partnership with Sugar&Spice had only heightened that. Rashad wasn't exactly a celebrity either, but he was well known enough in the media industry that people recognized his name, and were starting to recognize his face.

Put us two together, and ever since that interview video, almost six weeks ago, there had been quiet speculation about whether or not we were dating. Add the fact that I'd been seen out and about with Raisa (which meant I was cozying up to his sister, trying to get family approval), and our little teasing exchange from the video segment we'd done at the thrift shop (apparently I was flirting in public, to stake my claim), and we had supposedly become an "item".

BiShad, of all things, according to the people in my comments section, and our very own thread on a popular internet gossip forum.

"So... I guess I'll be the first to come out and ask the question everybody here wants to know... *are* you two an item?" Tanissa, the blogger who *created* the aforementioned gossip blocked our path, raising her mic in front of us as we stepped onto the red carpet area.

My eyes widened at the question, but I wasn't sure why.

I *knew* it was coming. It probably wasn't helping matters that we'd walked in together tonight. Although it was Sugar&Spice's event, and it made sense that we'd both *be* there, we maybe could have put some distance between us. But neither of us was thinking about that.

I glanced over at Rashad and subtly lifted an eyebrow, and he lifted his right back. Turning back to Tanissa, I shook my head as I smiled. "So, so sorry to disappoint anyone who was rooting for "BiShad", but that's not an actual *thing*. Rashad is an excellent photographer, and he and I have really great professional chemistry, but no, we definitely don't have any announcements to make. It's not like that."

Tanissa poked out her lip, flipping a handful of long, silky hair over her shoulder. "Come on, guys! As cute as you two look together right now? And we've *all* seen how this man makes you blush Bianca. Are you telling us we've been imagining things?"

I froze as Rashad snaked a hand around my waist, pulling me right up against him. When I looked up, there was a definitive glint of mischief in his eyes, and my heart began to race as I wondered what on earth he was about to do.

"Aiight, B," he said, using his free hand to grab mine, and raising it to his mouth. "I'm tired of us hiding... denying what we have." He planted a kiss on my fingers, then turned to Tanissa. "Scratch what she just said."

Eyes wide, she lifted her mic a little higher, and asked, "You're not playing with us are you, Mr. Martin?"

"Nah," he said, to my utter surprise. "This is my bae." With a wink, he leaned in, pressing his lips to the little spot just below my ear. After a week of no contact, his touch felt so good that I kind of forgot where I was, and closed my eyes. He lingered there for a full second before he pressed another kiss to the corner of my mouth, then pulled away.

My eyelids fluttered open, in time to see Rashad wink at me again before turning back to Tanissa, a completely serious expression on his face.

"Wow!" She looked between us, then over to her camera man. "Can I consider this an exclusive?" She directed that question at me, shoving her mic into my face.

"I... ummm"

"Nah, I'm pulling y'alls leg," Rashad chuckled, saving me from having to speak. I was still shocked at what he'd done, my skin was still tingling from that little kiss... I was in no shape to answer *anything*. "Since everybody wants to put us together, I'm having a little fun. The truth is, I think Bianca is sexy as hell, and incredible at what she does. I'd love to have a woman like this on my arm for real, but I guess I'll have to settle for working with her. And maybe I can convince her to dance with me a few times tonight."

Tanissa gave us a disbelieving smirk, then flipped her hair again. "Okay, okay now. I'm gonna take your word for it, but remember my motto... *these streets be watching, and these blogs be talking, chile.*"

And with that, Tanissa moved her attention to the people behind, effectively dismissing us. Rashad grabbed my hand to pull me into the party, but I tugged back, detouring until I found us an empty hall.

"What was *that*?" I asked, crossing my arms.

"What was what?"

I sucked my teeth, then pushed out a soft breath as he stepped closer, backing me against the wall as he entered my space. I looked up, meeting his eyes. "You *know* what Rashad. People were already whispering about us, and now…"

"You ashamed of me or something?" He gave me that cocky, half-dimpled smirk of his. "I'm not *that* bad, right?"

I scowled at him then, trying hard to keep a smile from tipping up the corners of my mouth. "No, it's… that felt like… too much."

Rashad drew his head back a little, and his indifferent expression shifted to apologetic. Putting a finger under my chin, he tipped it up, then gently pressed his lips to mine. "I'm sorry, B. I didn't think about that, I just… thought it would be funny."

"I know," I agreed, offering a reassuring smile. "And it *was*, really. I… I don't like *feeding* speculation, when *I'm* not even sure what's happening with us. I'm still adjusting to the idea of an *us* at all, and I know what putting a relationship on public display can do. I don't want it ruined before we… before we even have a *chance*. Does that make sense?"

He nodded, then pressed his lips to mine again. "Makes perfect sense. I will *never* do something like that again. Okay?"

"Okay."

"I'm sorry."

I grinned. "You said that already."

"Well I'm sayin' it again," he replied, gripping my waist.

"So say something different. Tell me something good."

"You *are* bae."

"I hate that word," I said, reaching up to cup his face. "It's right up there with saying something is *on fleek*."

Rashad chuckled, then moved his hands lower. "Yeah, well… Bae, your ass is *on fleek* in this dress."

"It *is* isn't it?"

"Look at *you*," he laughed, moving lower still, to cup and squeeze. "I thought you didn't like that word."

"It's fine when you're using it to compliment *me*."

»——«

"So is it true, or not?"

Fresh glass of champagne in hand, I turned to the source of the question to find Kieran standing behind me. He was in all white tonight as well, and looked good, but Rashad, in his black on black on black, still looked better.

Unfortunately for me, Rashad was already gone to catch his flight, and I still had twenty minutes left of my requisite two hours. I was *ready to go*, and a teensy bit cranky that when I *did* leave, it wouldn't be to lay up in Rashad's arms.

But I tried not to take that out on Kieran.

"Is *what* true?" I asked, taking a sip from my glass. I'd found a vacant table where I could sit and rest my feet, and Kieran took it upon himself to take the empty seat beside me.

"You and Rashad... I heard some people talking."

I raised an eyebrow at the question, wasn't at all surprised. Kieran hadn't been exactly subtle with his flirting, especially since we'd started meeting to discuss our project, which we were supposed to film next week.

"What makes you ask, Kieran?" I sat my champagne down on the table, careful not to spill, then turned back to him. "Why would you care about that?"

He shrugged, his voice dragging a little as he spoke. "Well... I thought it was obvious that I was hoping something might happen between me and you. But... I don't want to invade somebody else's territory, if you and Rashad—"

"*Invade someone else's territory*? Um... Kieran... I belong to myself, and myself only, no matter who I'm dating or not dating. The only thing you need to be concerned about is if *I'm* interested or not."

Kieran's eyes went wide. "My bad, Bianca. I didn't mean it like that."

Chill out, B.

I pushed out a heavy sigh, then shook my head. "I know you didn't, I'm tired, so I'm feeling a little off. Like how toddlers get cranky when they need a nap, you know? That's me right now."

Kieran laughed, though he seemed a little uneasy now.

"Yeah, I know that feeling. Nothing a good night of sleep can't fix. I live pretty close to here, if you need to…"

Ummm… excuse me?

"Uh, no thanks," I said, plastering on a smile as I stood, leaving my mostly-full glass of champagne there. I actually think I'm gonna head home."

"Do you need a ride? I can—"

I quickly shook my head. "Car service. I'm not that far."

"Oh, okay." He sounded disappointed as he stood. "Well… goodnight then, I guess." He pulled me into a hug that lingered a little too long, and I noticed then that his eyes were glossy, and he *smelled* like liquor.

Tipsy fool.

I had to ease away from him to end the embrace. I gave him a tight smile as I turned, heading for the exit as I pulled out my phone.

"Hey, Bianca!"

I turned around, and Kieran was still standing there, watching. "Yeah?"

"You never did answer my question… about you and Rashad."

Before I could help it, my face turned up in a scowl as I turned back to the main doors. "*Goodnight*, Kieran."

Shaking my head, I left, hoping that Kieran didn't embarrass himself or the magazine before the night was over. I doubted Cameron would take too kindly to a scandal, especially at *her* event.

Back at home, I stripped out of my dress and took a

shower, washed my hair, and scrubbed my face free of makeup. When I climbed into bed, I checked my phone, and saw that I had a text from Rashad.

"Just landed, bae. Turbulence on this flight was definitely NOT on fleek. – R.Martin."

I grinned at the screen, then typed back, **"Glad you made it safely. I hope you're going to bed soon. You've been traveling a lot, I know you're tired."**

"Yeah, I am," he messaged back. *"I'm about to catch a cab, get to this hotel and call it a night. Just wanted to let you know I was here. Goodnight B. - R.Martin."*

I thought about it for a few seconds, and then instead of typing a message in response, I pulled my tank top over my head and flipped on my bedside lamp. Making a kissy-face at the screen, I snapped a picture of myself and hit send.

"Come ooooonnnnn B! Why you gotta tease me like this? – R. Martin."

"Goodnight Shad."

"Goodnight, Satan. Yeah, Satan. No way would a child of God tease me like this. – R. Martin."

"SERIOUSLY?! You are sooo stupid, lol."

"You like it. – R. Martin."

"You right. Goodnight."

"Aiight then, B. Goodnight. – R.Martin."

I rolled over in bed with a contented sigh, intending to put my phone on the nightstand, but it chimed again. I turned the screen back on, expecting another text from Rashad, but instead it was an email.

I didn't recognize the address, so I used the preview

function to read the message without opening the full email.

"So... it's not "like that" with you and Rashad, huh? Sure looks "like that" to me."

Confused, I opened the message then, and saw that it contained a link to Tanissa's blog. I clicked the link, and my heart sank down to the pits of my stomach. The first thing I saw was a big, hi-definition picture of me, eyes closed, looking downright *blissful* as Rashad pressed his lips to my cheek.

Shit.

The comments section was already full of hype, and she had embedded a video of the minute-long "interview" as well. It wasn't like it was the biggest deal in the world, because Rashad and I were both single anyway, so it's not like we would get in trouble, but... *still.*

Much more concerning than this post was who had sent me that message.

eleven

. . .

bianca

I WOKE up feeling like life was good.

My career was going great, family was too. I was healthy, and *happy*. Rashad and I had a "thing". My heart felt really *full*, in a way it hadn't in a really long time.

I climbed out of bed and brushed my teeth and washed my face, then carefully untied the scarf from my hair. It had taken me forever to straighten, then curl my hair for the anniversary party last night, and I was trying to preserve that style as long as I could. I was still in the mirror with a comb when I thought about seeing how Rashad was faring that morning, after his late flight.

Retrieving my phone from the charger on my bedside table, the first thing I noticed was the *crazy* amount of notifications I had from my social media accounts, text messages from people I hadn't talked to in forever, emails, missed calls... all kinds of stuff.

Damn you Tanissa, I thought. I was pretty sure all of this sudden interest in talking to me was related to that little incident with Rashad last night. I cleared all of the notifications, then went to the missed calls, to make sure I hadn't missed anything *important*.

The six missed calls from Lauren got my attention.

I hit the dial-back button, but she didn't answer.

Probably in class.

If someone were sick, or hurt, she would have left a voicemail, so I didn't try to call back. I was going into my text messages when a tweet notification popped onto my screen. I started to ignore it, but my eyes snagged on part of the text, and I read the full thing.

"Edgy Good Girl" fashion blogger Bianca Bailey bares all! See the NSFW images here!

I narrowed my eyes at the screen. What the hell did they mean, *not-safe-for-work* images? I tapped to follow the link, which led to one of those awful blogs that made Tanissa's gossip site seem like motivational scripture. They spread the worst, unsubstantiated rumors, ruined careers, leaked private nude pictures… *wait a minute.*

My heart sank into the pit of my stomach as I waited for the page to load. I'd *known* better than to send those pictures to Rashad. Had his phone been hacked? Had *my* phone been hacked? Maybe *that's* why my notifications were blowing up. My face grew hot with embarrassment as I tried to tell myself that this would be fine. It would blow over, and people would forget. And I had great breasts. This wasn't the end of the world. There were worse things than people seeing me topless.

As soon as the page loaded... I realized how true that was.

There were *definitely* worse things than being seen nude from the waist up.

There weren't *just* pictures.

There was video... *multiple* videos, of me, having sex.

With... *Drew.*

My chest heaved up and down as my eyes roved over the images, from *years* ago, when he and I were together. Nausea swept my stomach as I watched him, behind me, on top of me, me on my knees for him, and *extremely* unaware that I was being filmed.

"I... ."

I *wanted* to speak out loud that I couldn't believe he would do this, but after everything... that wasn't even true. It was like an iron spike through the chest to realize that while I was disgusted, and embarrassed, incensed and offended by this violation... I wasn't surprised.

I wasn't *at all* surprised.

This was Drew, being exactly who he'd always been, and in that moment, I knew that the cryptic message from last night had absolutely been from him.

I didn't realize I was crying until teardrops dripped onto my screen, and I hastily wiped them away. Closing my eyes, I searched my mind, trying to figure out what the hell I was supposed to do about something like this. Who did I call first? A lawyer, the police? How the hell did I get this all pulled down?

Before I was even close to an answer, my phone rang again, and Cameron's assistant Denise's name popped up on my screen. With a jolt, I realized that of *course* they'd seen this. These images were probably being placed right beside images of me from last night at the Sugar and Spice event, being run with stories about how many different kinds of whores I was, with an *obvious* thing for handsome photographers.

She's probably calling to tell me they're stripping my entire existence from their website.

And who could blame them? Sugar&Spice had a reputation for fresh, quality content... not working with the next Kim Kardashian. Sex tape scandals weren't exactly their "thing".

The phone stopped ringing, then started again, and I took a deep breath, then answered. No point in delaying the inevitable.

"H-hello?" I asked, swallowing hard, trying to keep myself from sounding like I felt.

"Bianca... is that you?" Denise asked.

"Um, yes. It is."

"Good. Are you okay?"

Was I okay? There was no mistaking — they *definitely* knew about the videos.

"As well as could be expected, for what I woke up to," I answered honestly, wondering if maybe I *should* start sobbing. Perhaps they'd have mercy on me if they knew how pitiful—

"Cameron wants you to come into the office, to see her. As *soon* as you possibly can."

Seriously? I wasn't even gonna get a whole day before they got rid of me?

"Okay. I kinda have a crisis to deal with right now, can—"

"Make time, Bianca. Trust me on that."

With that, she hung up, offering no chance for a rebuttal, or for me to ask what she meant. I tossed the phone onto the bed, then scrubbed my hands over my face.

What the hell do I do?

I wouldn't google, I wouldn't check my comments, I wouldn't read my emails. I would *not* address this yet on my blog. I need to be *smart*, and careful about what I did, what I said, so that I didn't make this whole situation any worse. My family and my career were the two most important things in my life. I knew dad and Lauren weren't going to feel any differently about me, but something like this could destroy my reputation, and from there, my career.

Lauren still hadn't called back, I *definitely* wasn't about to call my dad... maybe Raisa would know? Picking up my cell again, I saw that I had a couple of missed calls from her, as well as a text asking if I were okay. There was *nothing* from Rashad, and I tried not to be concerned about that.

Maybe he was busy, or hadn't seen anything about what

was going on yet? He wouldn't be upset about this, or ignoring me... would he?

Before I could take *those* negative thoughts too far, my phone rang again, and this time, Raisa's name and smiling face flashed on the screen. I didn't hesitate to slide my finger across the screen to answer.

"Raisa, *help*," I said, as soon as I put the phone to my ear. "I don't know what to do, and I'm trying not to freak out, but I'm pretty sure I only have like five more minutes of calm left in me before I *blow*, and...*help!*"

"Okay, okay, okay, just... be easy." Raisa voice was comforting, but it did nothing to smooth over my frayed nerves. "Um... first of all, do you know who did this?"

"*Drew* did this. Because he's upset that I'm not running back, and I don't wanna be a part of his life, and I... he's probably upset about Rashad."

Raisa groaned. "The interview?"

"Yes. And...," I pushed out a heavy sigh, then flopped back on the bed. "And probably because I made a pissy comment about Rashad liking me, after I cursed him out as I was leaving the rehab center."

"So... this is revenge then."

"Basically."

"Good."

My face screwed up into a scowl. "*Good?*"

"Yes, *good*. There are rules against this shit, Bianca. You can nail his ass to the wall for something like this. Do you have a lawyer?"

"I've never *needed* one."

Raisa let out a dry chuckle. "Well... you do *now*. I'll talk to Gabe, ask if he knows anybody. And... it might be worth it to reach out to Cameron. S&S's name is getting thrown out a lot with these headlines... Maybe she can help, even if just for the sake of minimizing possible effects on the magazine?"

"Yeah, before or *after* she fires me because my goodies are all over the internet for everybody to see? This is... Raisa, I *can't* deal with this. How do I come back from the entire world seeing me face down ass up?"

Raisa was silent for a moment, and I could tell she was trying to find the right words. But... she really *didn't* know, and neither did I. *So what* that Drew could be punished for this? That did nothing to help the fact that something extremely private was now being used as entertainment for the world.

"I... don't know if this is any condolence, but you... at least you looked cute, right?"

"Bye Raisa."

"*Wait!* Wait, wait, wait! I'm trying to find even the tiniest possible bright spot here. I know this is a big deal, B."

Closing my eyes, I groaned. "I know, Rai. And I appreciate you, but there's no *bright spot* about this. I'm a *blogger*. A *YouTuber*. Every time I post something, I'll be reminding people, and the internet trolls will come out to play. I'm scared to even look at my blog and video comments right now, and *social media*? I already had people being gross, back when they only ever saw me fully clothed. Now? The *mama's basement* segments of twitter and facebook have probably turned me into some disgusting meme. Forget about it! I'm... gonna delete all of this stuff, and go into hiding or something. I've got a degree, I can probably find a job, if none of the interviewers have seen me with Drew's di—"

"Girl are you crazy?" Raisa's suddenly sharp tone made me stop my tirade to listen. "Don't you friggin' *dare* delete anything. Don't you *dare* let him take away something that means *everything* to you! Hell no!"

Sitting up, I remained silent while her words sunk in. This was probably why he did this in the first place, wanting me to be overwhelmed, and so embarrassed that I would shrink and hide. But... *screw him.*

"I...," I pushed out a heavy sigh before I continued. "I guess you're right. I can't let him win like this. I've gotta go, Raisa. Cameron summoned me to her office, and if I'm gonna salvage my career from this at all, I need to talk to her. Even if she does fire me... maybe she can still recommend something. And... thank you, for talking me back from a cliff."

"You're welcome, beautiful girl. Good luck."

As soon as we hung up, I remembered that I hadn't asked about Rashad, and his lack of a text or phone call to me. But... I couldn't worry about it right now. He was probably busy, and I had something to do anyway.

I got myself out of bed, got dressed, put on the biggest sunglasses I had to hide my face, and then... I went to see Cameron.

»——«

It felt like everybody was staring at me.

I knew they weren't, knew that I was being ridiculous, but from my building to the cab, from the cab to the Sugar&Spice offices, it felt like all eyes were on me, and all eyes had seen me naked, in what was supposed to be a private act of intimacy.

The door to Cameron's office opened as I approached, and Kieran stepped out, closing it behind him. I gave him my customary smile in greeting, but he seemed startled by my presence, and froze in the middle of the hall.

"B-Bianca... hi. Good morning."

Somehow, I could tell he was having a *very* hard time keeping his eyes on my face. I closed my arms protectively around my body, even though I was fully covered.

"Good morning, Kieran." I started to walk around him, but stopped when I was a few feet away to look back. "Hey... I'm sure you've probably heard about, or... *seen*, this little scandal, and I know we have a project together. *If* I'm kept on this blogger experience with the magazine, I want you to know that I *won't* let this prevent me from doing my part. You shouldn't have to carry that weight by yourself because of my personal mishaps."

Kieran's lips parted, and then he lifted a hand, scratching his head as he shifted uncomfortably on his feet. "Umm... about that... I think it's probably best if we... *don't* do our project together. I actually just got done speaking to Cameron about it."

"Oh?" I swallowed hard, trying to hinder the tears pricking my eyes as I realized what he was saying.

"Yeah… I've… I've gotta be protective of my brand, I know you understand that Bianca. My image has to stay clean, and—"

"I'm… *dirty*. My asshole ex boyfriend completely violates my privacy, and *I'm* dirty. Got it." Shaking my head, I turned away to head into the office, but Kieran caught my hand.

"I'm *sorry* Bianca," he said, and I could see in his eyes that he meant it, but that didn't make the situation any less hurtful. "You have to understand, I—"

I waved my free hand, brushing away his words. "I get it, Kieran."

He gave the hand he was holding a gentle squeeze. "Thank you. And… I'm sorry this happened to you. Maybe once it all blows over, we can get together… have a nice dinner, drinks?"

Tipping my head to the side, I surveyed him for a moment as I tried to figure out what, exactly, he was saying. He gave a creepy little smile, and I realized then what he meant.

Snatching my hand away, I took a step back. "So… your little clean-cut sports image can't be tainted by a fashion blogger with a sex tape, but I'm good enough to sneak around with? You are *so* full of shit."

"Wait a minute, Bianca. *Come on*. We both know you're

gonna be un-dateable for minute behind something like this. What man is gonna be okay with being able to see the woman he's interested in get shoved into the mattress by another du—"

Kieran didn't get a chance to finish that statement before my hand connected with his face. Heat and pain radiated through my palm, but the red handprint spreading over Kieran's light golden-brown skin made it absolutely worth it.

"Your wack ass better *never* find a reason to speak to me again."

Before he could respond, I was on the other side of the door, and immensely grateful for the small waiting area and reception desk that separated me from Cameron. The reception desk was vacant, so I was able to take a moment and collect myself, so I wouldn't face Cameron Taylor with tears in my eyes.

How *dare* Kieran make it seem like I was some... *undesirable*, as if...

What if that's why Rashad hasn't called?

My eyes went wide as I considered that possibility. One day they're talking about me and him together, and he's kissing me, and telling anyone who saw that video that he wanted me on his arm. The next, people are watching me have sex with someone else. Kieran was actually right. As territorial and egotistical as men tended to be... it made sense.

Why *wouldn't* Rashad be embarrassed, why *would* he call? We weren't even officially dating, so it wasn't like he owed me anything. He was a single man, and I... *was* undateable.

"Bianca? You're here to see Cameron, right?"

I looked up, and pulled myself from my thoughts to see Denise standing at the door to Cameron's private office. Straightening up, I hastily wiped tears from my face.

"Yes. I am, if now is a good time."

Denise smiled. "Of course sweetie. Come on back."

Taking a deep breath, I followed Denise's directions as she led me inside, but then stepped out, closing the door behind me. Cameron looked up from something on her computer to give me a comforting smile, then beckoned me closer.

"Bianca Bailey, come on in and sit down."

I did as I was told, taking a seat in a plush, comfortable chair right across from her desk. Cameron's office was mostly white, but accented with lush purples and blacks that were somehow soothing and warm. Or maybe... that was just Cameron. Now that I was sitting in front of her, I felt less anxious, but still uncertain about what was going to happen.

"So... are you okay?" she asked, relaxing back in her chair as she waited for my answer.

I thought about it for a moment and nodded, but then changed my mind and shook my head. "I... I guess I don't really know, honestly. I've purposely avoided reading anything, or talking to anyone except good friends and family, but I know that at some point, I'll have to stop ignoring it. It *has* to be addressed."

"You're right." Cameron sat up, folding her hands together and resting them on the desk as she leaned forward. "It *will* have to be addressed, but the key is doing it in the right way, so that we mitigate the risk."

"... We?" I said cautiously, my heart racing as a little spark of hope cropped up. "So... you're *not* terminating my internship because of this?"

Cameron's face balled into a scowl. "*What*? Absolutely *not*! Bianca... you're a victim here, and I have no plans to leave you flailing in the wind. Especially not when you're connected to Sugar&Spice. No, you'll have my full support. I've actually already taken the liberty of contacting the law firm I use, Pritchard, Graham & Whitaker. One of the lawyers in particular, Gabi Lucas-Whitaker, has experience in dealing with things like this, and she's agreed to set up a phone call with you, since they're located in Atlanta. They're waiting on a *yes* from you to move forward."

"*Yes*," I exclaimed as I sat up, hanging nearly on the edge of my seat. "Yes, *yes*. Thank you *so* much Ms. Taylor, I—"

"Who?" Cameron clenched her jaw, but the corners of her mouth twitched.

"*Cameron*. Thank you, Cameron."

She smiled then. "It's not a problem at all. This type of thing really bothers me, and it seems to be increasingly popular these days. A bad thing, but also a good thing, because our laws seem to be catching up. At minimum, the punishment can be fines, but I've got a feeling Gabi will want to pursue jail time. And definitely a civil suit as well. We've just gotta figure out the responsible party."

"Drew Randle," I said immediately. "And he shot that video without my permission. I've... taken pictures, but *never* during sex, and *never* video. I never agreed to that."

"Okay. We'll tell the lawyers all of that, and go from there, alright? I know this seems really awful right now, but we're gonna get this cleaned up, and you'll be fine. Sugar&Spice is on your side."

"Yeah... except my supposed partner." I blew out a heavy sigh, and Cameron rolled her eyes.

"Are you referring to Kieran Duke?" she asked, then rolled her eyes harder when I confirmed. "I would not be concerned about him. I *did* let him pull out of your joint project, because I understand his fears for his career, but... I've made it clear from the beginning that S&S is about being a team player. If he can't take this as an opportunity to stand up for one of his peers, and speak out against a pretty gross violation of your privacy.... He may not be S&S material. His stint here may be very short-lived. But enough about him, right? Keep doing what you're doing. Take a little break, visit family, talk to friends. Stay off the internet. I'm gonna have my PR team come up with a plan for you, okay?"

"Okay. Again... thank you so much!"

"Again, not a problem. You're good at what you do, and have an obvious passion for it. I *want* to see you succeed. This mess is a hiccup. A... large hiccup, but a hiccup nonetheless. They come and they go, but they never stick around too long, right?"

"Right."

She gave me a smile, and I smiled right back, then stood to leave. Cameron stood as well, and before I knew what was happening, she'd pulled me into a hug, and my eyes started watering. I gave an assenting nod to her whispered *you're gonna be okay* before showing myself out of her office. My shoulders sagged with relief as I stood at Denise's desk to arrange a meeting with Gabi Lucas-Whitaker, and the magazine's PR team.

With that taken care of, I pulled out my phone as I headed to the elevators that would lead me back downstairs. I immediately dismissed all of the notifications without looking at them, and tried to call Lauren again. When she didn't answer, I took a deep breath, then sat down on a vacant bench in the hall and called my dad, who picked up on the first ring.

"I'm gonna *kill* that boy!" was the first thing out of his mouth, no attempt to say "hello". His voice shook with anger as he launched into a tirade about how he'd never liked Drew, knew he was no good, how I should have known better, etc. A few of his points about the way *I* had dealt with Drew stung, but I listened anyway.

Even though he'd been more than a little bit absent because of his job, my father had never, ever wavered in caring for me and Lauren. Even when we "messed up" — me being involved with Drew, her getting pregnant at sixteen — there had never been a moment where either of his felt his disappointment outweighed his love. It was the kind of trait I should have noticed was conspicuously absent in Drew — but I'd known, and certainly benefited from it with Rashad.

I devoted a few minutes to calming my father down, making him promise not to kill anyone, and assuring him that I was okay.

But… I wasn't sure if that was true.

Even though I was absolutely relieved that I wasn't losing my opportunity with Sugar&Spice, and that they would actually *help*, just like I told Raisa… nothing could be done about the fact that it was out there, had been for at least a few hours. Everybody who *cared* to see it, had definitely seen.

And then… there was Rashad.

Once I was off the phone with my dad, I navigated to Rashad's number and stared at it on my screen. I wanted to call, badly, but… I didn't even know what to say. And more than that… I didn't want to face a possible rejection.

Shaking my head, I pushed the phone back into my purse and stood up, turning the corner for the elevator. It chimed as I approached, and my steps faltered. I didn't want to run into anyone else, I wanted to get home, crawl under my covers, and pretend today hadn't happened. I held my breath as the doors opened, and then…

"Rashad?"

He had his face pointed down at his phone, tapping

away, but he looked up when I said his name. There was a full second where he just... *looked* at me, and a million negative things ran through my mind. Obviously his phone was working since he was using it now. Was he avoiding me? Was he disappointed to see me? Was he grossed out? Those questions bounced in my head at hyper-speed, but then... Rashad's arms were around me. He put his hand against the back of my head, pulling it against his chest as he drew me close, tightening his hold.

"I've been looking for you, B," he said, pressing his lips to my forehead. "I had to call Raisa to find out where you were. Why aren't you answering your phone?"

Stepping back, I shook my head as tears sprang to my eyes, unannounced. "Too much going on. I turned the volume off, and I've been clearing the notifications. I checked to see if you'd called this morning though, and there was nothing from you."

"I was on the plane. I caught a flight as soon as I saw this shit, hoping that I would get to you before *you* saw it. I've known you for seven Mondays, and I know you've slept late at least five of those. I was hoping that would be the case today."

I swallowed hard, hoping that my voice wouldn't sound too choked with emotion. "So... you left a job, to get on a plane to come back here because...why?"

"Because I thought you might..." He stopped, swiping his hands over his face before tucking them into his pockets. "B... I'm not trying to freak you out, aiight? I know last night, you were talking about not rushing it, and not being comfortable with the idea of an *us*, and—"

"What are you *talking* about, Shad? Just *say* it."

"*Okay.* Like...," he pushed out a heavy sigh, then shook his head. "I... I was up early. *Really* early, because the shoot I was doing was at four in the morning. We finished for the day, and packed up, and I was back in my hotel room by seven, which is when I saw everything. The *first* thought that came to my mind was... *I have to get to Bianca. She might need me.* So... I got on a plane. To get to you... in case you needed me. And I know that's corny, and dramatic, and too soon to even be thinking about shit like—"

"I *do* need you," I said, stepping forward to grab handfuls of his shirt to get his attention. "If it's too soon, it just *is*, but... I'm not okay. The situation will be handled, Drew will be handled, *this* will be okay later, but right now... *I'm not.* And I *do* need you."

He smiled at me, and then cupping my face between his hands, he planted a kiss on my lips, in full view of anyone who happened to walk by. But in that moment, I really didn't care who knew. I felt... *silly*, really, for ever even considering that Rashad's reaction would have been anything different. Of course he wasn't embarrassed, or disgusted by me. We may have been young, but Rashad was... *grown.* For real *grown*, and secure enough in himself that it was okay for me to be *me*... mistakes and all.

»——«

"Are you trying to turn into a prune?"

I opened my eyes to see Lauren standing over me, a towel in one hand, and an unopened jar of caramel apple pie Talenti in the other.

I'd been in Rashad's bathtub for the last hour, soaking away my worries while Lauren waited for me in the living room. He'd had to fly back to finish his project, and would be gone for the next week, but had agreed to me hanging around until he got back. I knew it was a strange request on my behalf, but being in *his* space, with his scents, and *his* pillows, just…. made it feel a little less lonely.

Lauren's presence helped as well. After she'd gotten out of class and could finally return my calls, she'd taken off for a day to come and see me. So when I'd disappeared into the bathroom shortly after she arrived, she was annoyed to say the least. But I *needed* that soak, to cleanse my spirit. Or… something like that. After speaking with lawyers, and PR people, and police, my brain was *fried.*

"You know you're gonna be fine, right?" Lauren asked, when I was finally out of the tub, and we were sitting at Rashad's kitchen table, sharing the tub of gelato. "I know you're avoiding reading anything about it, but for the most part, everybody is talking about how *hot* you look, and how stupid Drew is. I was watching Arnez & Arizona earlier, and you know how *harsh* they usually are, right?"

Arnez & Arizona were a gay man/ best girlfriend vlogger duo who talked about everything from fashion to celebrity gossip to movies and music. They were known for their over the top personalities, and a tendency to lean more toward the "mean" side.

"Here," Lauren continued, pulling out her phone. "Let me show you."

She navigated to YouTube on her phone and pulled up Arnez and Arizona's latest episode. She moved the progress bar to a point a few minutes in, then hit play.

"Okaaaay," Arizona's perky voice chirped from the phone's speakers. "So, the internet is all abuzz this morning with news of a certain *little miss perfect —*"

"And *friend of the show!*" Arnez chimed in.

Arizona laughed. "Yes, and *friend of the show,* because y'all know Arnez *loves* him some Bianca Bailey, honey."

"I sure damned *do,* that bitch can put an outfit together from a pillowcase and some toothpicks and *slay* your entire life, chile."

"We get it Arnez."

"Snatch your whole wig, girl. Edges gone, and the middle too."

"We *get it,*" Arizona said, shooting him a playful scowl. "Anyway, fashion blogging's favorite brown girl was caught on camera taking the "D", and although she's *friend of the show...* y'all know we gotta talk about it, right?" She looked directly at the camera, smirking like she was really waiting for an answer, then turned to Arnez. "We'll start with you, since you're the Bianca super-fan around here. What did *you* think?"

Arnez took a deep, dramatic breath, then placed his hand to his chest. "Well, honey you know I was *distraught* to find out that my sweet, put-together Bianca would *ever* associate herself with the likes of a *Drew Randle*. But it seems to me like he was nothing more than a bad memory, because the other night, Ms. Bailey almost swooned out of her fly-ass Giuseppe's when a *different* fine-ass photographer was flirting with her at the Sugar&Spice event."

"Mmmhmmm," Arizona agreed. "Which is probably why the ex decided he wanted to show out. I detect some jealously there, but I really wish he'd thought twice, because did you see that little broken churro of a dick? Poor Bianca, and he was really waving that lil thangalang around like he was proud! He couldn't have had those parts cropped out if he was tryna embarrass somebody?"

Arnez broke into giggles. "Chile, he's already had enough *cropped*, from the looks of it. Which is probably why Bianca looked so *bored* in those videos. I mean *really*? If you ask me, *he's* the one who looks bad, if you're going to town on somebody, working up a sweat, and her eyes are on the TV instead of rolling back in her head."

"Hello?! The girl laughed at a joke, and she was watching SNL, so you know she must have been *real* bored, cause that shit isn't even funny!"

"Girl," Arnez started, "How about there's more chemistry and heat in that kiss on the cheek from Rashad Martin than any of those videos that it doesn't even look like she was aware of?"

Arizona gave a loud whoop, then clapped. "And that *look* she gave him after, *my God*! I got hot like *I* was about to get some! That was that "I'm *draining* your nuts when we get outta here" look. Just come wherever you want to, all over me, all in my hair, rub it in."

Arnez stared at Arizona for a long moment, then looked back at the camera with several slow blinks. "And there, ladies and gentlemen, is your proof that Miss Arizona is a stone cold freak. Did you see how excited she got, how *far* she took it just then?"

"Whatever Arnez, I know how *you* do," Arizona laughed. "In any case… we aint gonna lie like we didn't see it, but Bianca if you're watching, I do hate it happened to you, since knowing you, I'm pretty positive you didn't want something like that out. But you look cute in it though."

"Real cute," Arnez added. "Fine as fuck."

"Bad as hell, girl. So you'll be okay chile!"

Arnez nodded. "Sure will. And as a matter of fact, we're gonna give out our award early in today's episode. Our "You Better *Werk Bitch*" award goes to Bianca Bailey, for always being a class act, and for looking good in your little secret sex tape. And our "Ugh, Bitch, Why Are You SO Damned *Wack*" award goes to Drew Randle, for being… *wack*. Aint no secret that his ass leaked those tapes, and he's so stupid for doing it *right* after we watched BiShad being all adorable. You're jealous, Drew, and it ain't cute. Just… *stop*."

"Agreed." Arizona shook her head at the screen, then flipped over her next topic card, and Lauren turned off the video.

"See what I mean? *He* looks stupid, not you. All of this will blow over, and you'll be fine."

I sat back, twirling my spoon between my fingers. "If you say so, Lauren. I mean... it's awesome to have support, but... I feel helpless."

"You're not helpless at all," Lauren shook her head, giving me a stern look like *she* was the big sister. "You're beautiful, and strong, and inspirational, and *so* cool. Do you realize how much I look up to you, Bianca? You're only twenty-five, and aside from this scandal, you've got your shit together, with a successful, self-made career. I wanna be like *you* when I grow up.'

I shook my head, then leaned forward, dropping the spoon onto the table before I covered Lauren's hands with mine. "Sis... don't look up to me, okay? I... I haven't done anything special enough for that. If *anything*... hell, I should be looking up to *you*."

"For *what*," Lauren sucked her teeth. "Ohhh, a broke teen mom. Yeah, that's something to *aspire* to."

She rolled her eyes, and tried to pull her hands away, but I held tight. "Lauren...do *not* talk down about yourself like that. I'm serious. *You're* the inspiration. I'm the screw-up here."

"Whatever, B. I don't feel like doing this with you today."

"Well, too bad. Cause we're about to," I said, squeezing her hands. "Sis... you know how I kinda... disappeared while you were pregnant?"

She nodded. "Yeah. You were stuck up under Drew."

"Yeah, well... that's only *part* of the truth." I swallowed hard, then continued. "Lauren... I had a pregnancy scare, right around the time you came to me and told me *you* were pregnant. I was... I was *terrified*, because if I'm honest with myself, I knew back then that I needed to let that relationship go. But... a *baby*? That's *permanent*. But you... you handled yourself, with such dignity, and grace. Way more than I had. You admitted that you'd made contraception mistakes, you accepted responsibility, you worked with Harper's dad, and all of the parents, you made a plan. And *I*... I was *scared*."

"You don't think I was *scared*?" she exclaimed, shaking her head. "I was terrified too Bianca, I didn't know what I was doing!"

"But you made the best of it," I countered. "You still are. You're kicking ass at school, gonna graduate early, get a great job. You're a *wonderful* mother to Harper, and you're mature, and you're grounded, and you're like... the best sister ever. *You* are the inspiration, Lauren. Not me. If I *had* been pregnant, I would *not* have had Drew's child. I probably would have hated myself forever for it, but at least I wouldn't have been tied to him. And every time I saw you, I was... jealous, that you could handle it so maturely, when you're six years younger. And guilty, that I wasn't willing to make the same sacrifice you were. So... don't look up to me. I'm not anybody to look up to."

Lauren stared at me for a moment, then sat back, brushing her hair away from her face. "Why wouldn't you tell me something like this?"

"I didn't tell *anybody*. Drew doesn't even know, thank God. I... like I said, I felt *bad* about it. And I shouldn't have distanced myself from you, but... my head was all messed up then. But... that did make me realize that I needed to get away from him. The thought of bringing a child into the world with a manipulative, narcissistic father like that... is something out of a horror movie to me."

Silence hung in the air for a long moment before I spoke again. "I love you, baby sis. And I know I've said this a billion times, but... I'm *so* sorry I wasn't there for you."

"Oh *please*, Bianca," she said, waving me off. "You've done *way* too much for me *since* then for me to trip about that. I just wish you'd told me. But... for what it's worth, I *still* think you're an inspiration. You recognized that you were in a toxic relationship, got out, turned your life around. You're *still* successful, no matter how hard he tried to tear you down. *Still* trying, actually. Have you called and cursed him out yet?"

I shook my head. "No. Cameron, the PR people, the police, the lawyers, everybody told me not to. They said it's best to handle everything through official channels, so... that's what I'm doing."

Honestly, it killed me to not hear from his mouth *why* he'd done this to me, even though I had a good idea. Control issues, jealousy, resentment, and that *crazy ass* mama of his, who I was almost *sure* had something to do with it.

Lauren stood up, coming around the table to pull me into a hug. "Good girl," she said.

"Good girl? You're forgetting which sister is which again?" I laughed, pinching her arm.

"*Never*. Just making sure you know *I* approve. I love you sis."

I smiled, then pulled her into another hug. "And I love you."

twelve

. . .

rashad

I SHOULD KILL THIS MOTHERFUCKER.

That was the thought that *kept* running through my head as I sat at the end of a table full of people, glaring at Drew, who was a couple of tables away.

After I was sure Bianca was okay, I *had* to fly back to the middle of nowhere to finish my assignment, and then the next flight, two days later, was to a photography conference in California. The conference wasn't something I *had* to do, but I went every year, and usually learned a lot. But *this* year... Bianca was hurting. I could have flown back home... maybe *should* have flown back home, but I was *hoping* — praying, even — that I would run into Drew.

Because I should probably kill him.

The fact that he'd violated Bianca's privacy, tried to embarrass her and destroy her reputation, thereby ruining her career, which was *so* important to her... that was enough to put thoughts of choking him on my mind. But then I thought about it a little more, and started feeling like wait a minute… this shit was a jab at *me* too, as if he were saying to me *look what I did with your girl.*

No, we hadn't established any titles, but whatever. When it came to *this* shit, yeah, she was my girl, and he'd fucked with her, so he'd fucked with *me*. And he *really* had the nerve to walk into this conference with his chest puffed out, like he was somebody, or had done something to be envied.

Fuck him.

The *problem* was that Bianca had asked me not to do anything. She let me rant about Drew for damn near twenty minutes, and then laid her hand on my chest and asked me to chill. That was the *only* reason I hadn't sought him out, but now that he was *right here in my face,* grinning and laughing and living it up. Bianca couldn't even comfortably walk down the street without wondering whether the people she shared the sidewalk with had seen her naked, but *this* motherfucker was out here being breezy.

It didn't sit right with me.

But… *damn it,* I told Bianca I would chill.

So I did.

Even though it was burning me up.

I sat in on a few sessions, but I couldn't even focus knowing that Drew was actually enjoying his life. And then some dumb ass stopped me in the hall, and asked me about the shit with Bianca. After *that* virtual ass-handing, I headed to the bathroom, hoping that whoever that idiot stranger was, I hadn't cursed out somebody important. Important or not though, it tanked my mood even further, to the point that when I was in the bathroom handling my business and Drew walked in, I was honestly ready to snap.

I looked up from washing my hands, and our eyes met in the mirror. I shook my head and went back to what I was doing, because I remembered what I told Bianca, that I would chill.

Do not say anything to me, motherfucker. Do not say anything to me. I will punch your teeth down your goddamn throat if you say anything. Don't fucking say anything to me.

"It's been a minute, bruh."

Goddamn, he said something.

I turned off the water and turned to get a paper towel, but didn't bother pretending like I hadn't heard him. I looked right at his punk ass, hoping that the scowl on my face was enough to send the *if you value your life, shut the fuck up* message, but Drew grinned, stepping in front of me as I moved toward the exit door.

"Ah, come on Rashad," he said, looking smug. "Don't tell me you're upset about those little videos."

"Get your ass out of my way, Drew. You don't want this problem right now, I promise you." I tried to move around him, but he sidestepped me again, holding up his hands. And he was *still* wearing that little pissy smirk.

"I haven't even showed the *real* deal stuff yet. Have you had a piece of—"

Whatever he was saying, I punched that shit right back into his mouth, then snatched him up by the collar, making sure to smack his head against the door as I slammed him against it.

"Do *not* fucking talk to me like we're homeboys," I growled, moving my hands to his throat. "We're not cool, bruh. Especially not after you pulled this shit with B. I'm gonna tell you this *one* time: *don't fuck with her again.* Don't release a picture, a text message, nothing. Don't call, don't email, don't text, don't send a carrier pigeon. Don't watch her videos, don't go to her blog, don't look at her, don't say her name, don't even *think* about her. The *only* reason I'm not about to fuck your punk ass up is because you aren't worth my freedom. Do something else, and I might have to use some new math to make that decision. You feel me?"

I released my hold on him, and he shoved me away. "Whatever man. Empty threats don't mean shit to me," he said, wiping blood from the corner of his mouth. "Tell that *bitch* Bi—"

"You really think I'm playing don't you?" I snapped, grabbing him by the neck and pushing him into the wall again as I squeezed. He tried to swing on me, but I easily dodged it, then hit him with a body blow to the gut, followed by another jab to the face before I grabbed him by the collar and tossed him to the floor, not caring that his head bounced against the tile *hard* as he fell. "Nobody is *threatening* you. I'm telling you what's gonna happen."

I knew better than to turn my back on a dude like that, but he stayed where he was on the floor, groaning like I'd really kicked his ass. I really *should* have kicked his ass.

"I'm calling the police, motherfucker," he sputtered from the floor, rolling onto his back.

Shaking my head, I grabbed the door handle. "I bet you are. And I'll tell them that you walked in to the bathroom starting bullshit while I was minding my business. You got in my way while I was trying to leave, so I had to defend myself. We'll see who they believe, right?"

I let the door slam behind me, and then... I left the conference feeling *good*. My fist was a little tender, but that was okay, because fuck that dude. Next time he got photographed, it would be with a black eye and a fat lip — neither of which was my fault, if you asked *me*. I was *trying* to not have to hit him.

When I got back home after a six hour flight, I was happy to find Bianca in my bed, sound asleep. Like... *giddy* about it. If she was comfortable enough to sleep in my bed, be in my space when I wasn't even there... that meant she was comfortable with *me*.

It was well after midnight, so I took a shower, then climbed into bed, wrapping an arm around her to pull her close. I drifted off almost immediately, but woke up a few hours later — I *think* — with Bianca straddling my legs, leaning forward to press her lips to my neck.

My dick sprang to attention in my boxers as she planted juicy kisses in a trail, from my neck, to my chin, and then to my lips. In the dim early-morning light, our eyes met, and she gave me a sleepy smile.

"Good morning," she murmured against my lips as she reached between us, to push my boxers down.

I pushed myself up, to help her, and then returned her grin. "Good morning to you too… what time is it?"

"Time for… *this*."

I groaned as she lowered herself onto me, surrounding me in warmth, and wetness, and… *heaven*. I ran my hands up her naked body as she began to move, rolling her hips against me in loose, rhythmic waves.

"I *missed* you." She whispered that against my neck as my fingers gripped her thighs, then she sat up, giving me a glorious view as she rode me. "I needed this."

"Did something happen?"

She shook her head, then balanced herself with her hands on my chest, still moving. "Nothing you don't know about already. Released a statement, talked to the police again. Done everything I can, and now… I wait. And the waiting is…." She stopped for a moment, shook her head again, then began to ride me harder.

"Hey," I said, bringing my hands up to her breasts to caress and stroke her nipples. She closed her eyes, then moved her hands over mine, urging me to squeeze harder as she began to grind on my lap. "It's gonna be fi—"

"*Don't* say that." Her eyes snapped open, and she went still. "I'm tired of everybody saying that *it's gonna be fine*, when it's not *them*. It's not *their* naked ass on display for the entire world to see. You don't know how it—" Her voice broke, and she moved her hands back to my chest before meeting my gaze again. "I... I'm sorry. I don't mean to be a bitch to you, I—"

Before she could finish getting that out, I sat up, cupping her face in my hands to kiss her. I probed her mouth with my tongue, and she opened up, relaxing against my chest as I wrapped her in my arms. Salty tears began to spill down her cheeks as our tongues played, and by the time we finally pulled away, her face was completely wet.

I used a finger under her chin to turn her face up to mine in the growing sunlight. "You're angry," I said, wiping away her tears with my thumbs. "And embarrassed, and hurting, and confused, and... I *get* it, B." I glanced at the bruised knuckles on my right hand and nodded. "I *definitely* get it."

"It's not an excuse, though."

I dipped my head. "You're right... it's *not* an excuse. But it damn sure is a good reason."

For a long moment, Bianca kinda stared at me, and then fresh tears welled in her eyes as she shook her head. She snaked her arms around me and laid her head down, burying her face in my neck. "I don't understand why you're so... *good* to me."

I chuckled, then kissed the top of her head. "I explained that shit weeks ago, B. I'm doing what feels natural, being honest with you, trying to make you happy. There's nothing exceptional about that... or *shouldn't* be."

"You... talk such a good game," Bianca said, sitting up so she could meet my gaze. "And... I don't mean that negatively, I *swear*. I think you really mean it when you say these things to me, but I can't help wondering if... I mean, are you saying these things — even if it's unconscious —to appease me? To charm me? To keep me wrapped up in... whatever this is we're doing? I know it's probably not fair to you, to doubt you based on *my* past experience, but... like I said... this sounds way too good to *not* be game."

I cocked an eyebrow, angling my head to the side in disbelief. "Bianca... if I wanted pussy, I could have *gotten* pussy, with a lot less hassle and frustration. I'm not a ... *game-running* type of dude. I may play around, but I'm always honest, always up front with my intentions, and *always* mindful of not fucking around with people's feelings, cause I don't want anybody fucking with mine. I don't know what to *say* to make you comfortable enough that you don't have to be guarded with me. I can only... *do*. My dad didn't teach me game, he taught me *respect*. I don't know anything about playing games."

I cupped her face again, and pressed another kiss to her lips. "This is about to sound sappy, I know, but... he also taught me about a woman who I wouldn't be able to avoid if I tried. Somebody that would have my head messed up, and my heart wrapped up, for reasons I couldn't understand or explain. That's *you*, B. Even when you're being a bitch — *your words*— everything about you appeals to me. You frustrate me, and you confuse me, but you also intrigue me, and draw me in, and that's where I can see that you're funny, and smart, and beautiful, and ... shit, I don't know," I chuckled. "I would tell you to stop being so fucking difficult, but at this point, I think it's part of who you are. And I'm okay with that... Aiight?"

"*Aiight,*" she whispered against my lips as she leaned in. "Thank you... for taking such good care of me. And... a whole lot of other stuff I'm not gonna say right now, cause I think we've already reached peak sappiness for the day."

I sucked my teeth. "Oh, so *you* get the romantic declaration, but I don't?"

"Is that what that was?" Bianca teased, giving me a big smile. "I didn't realize."

"Cause you're a *hater.*"

Bianca lifted her hands to my face, and gave me a look that was... beyond what I could explain. I *felt* it, but... I couldn't explain. "A *hater? Never.* Not of *you. You* have... given me hope. Given me... *optimism. Cautious* optimism... but still. And there's *your* romantic declaration."

"That's all I get? *Damn.*"

She giggled. "That's... all you get *for now.* I'm... *trying.*"

"Well then I'll take that. C for effort."

"A *C?!*" she asked, drawing back with a big smile on her face. "I can't get at least like... a *B,* on the strength of you *still* being hard, and *still* being inside me right now?"

"Come on, Bianca. You started this emotional ass conversation, and haven't moved in like ten minutes. If you wanted a better grade, you should've kept riding."

"Mmmm, is it too late to raise my grade?" she asked, biting her lip as she positioned her hands on my shoulders for balance.

"Not yet... but you better get to work now." I swatted

her ass, and she yelped, then giggled as she began rolling her hips on me again.

She gave me a wicked little grin, then put her arms around my neck as she sank all the way down. "Like this?"

"*Hell yes*," I growled in her ear, gripping her thighs. "And if you want extra credit…"

"Give you lips?"

I chuckled, then lowered my mouth to hers. "That's right. *Gimme lips.*"

»—«

Bianca.

»—«

"You can't tell people you don't believe in love.

Well… wait, let me rephrase: You *shouldn't* tell people you don't believe in love.

Cause as soon as you do, they wanna break you down, figure you out, *get to the root of what makes you so bitter,* as if not buying into love as the pinnacle of relational happiness automatically means you must have endured some type of tragic heartbreak.

And… they're probably right. I can't speak for anyone else, but when I looked back over the last two months of my life… it was certainly true for me. I was past the point of feeling down about who I was, had grown beyond my own self doubt. *Bianca* was dope. I *believed* that.

The problem lied with my ability to *want* romantic

love in my life. Not because I didn't feel like I deserved it, but… more because I didn't really understand the function. I said it before… I've felt love. Family, and friends, I *knew* what that was like. The feeling of someone being there for you, lifting you up, allowing you to be yourself, flaws and all, and loving you anyway. Someone that you can hang with, laugh with, someone who makes you feel completely comfortable… I hadn't experienced that with Drew, only infatuation, so I didn't understand that all of those things were supposed to come with romantic love too.

Until Rashad.

He came… out of nowhere, on my damned nerves *hard*. And… he blew my mind. *Two months*. So, *so* much has happened, in so little time, but I guess that's the way it goes, right? Just up and hits you out of nowhere… a complete surprise. *Serendipity* is the word, I think. A completely sappy, romance novel type of thing, and it… it happened to *me*, of all people.

Little old bitter Bianca… wasn't quite so bitter anymore.

I don't want to say that I *love* Rashad, because it feels too *soon* for that, you know? Who does that? It's ridiculous! But… I can't say that I *don't*. Even thinking about denying it makes my stomach hurt a little, so… maybe I'm in denial. But that's okay. We're taking our time, cause we have it. We're still really young, so…there's no rush.

But he *did* call me his "girl" in front of Cameron, and

at dinner with his parents, which I didn't know was happening until they walked into Honeybee and sat down at the table with me, Rashad, Raisa, and Gabe. So… there's *that*.

Maybe I should just say it… I love Rashad. Maybe… I should say it out loud. Maybe… it *won't* be something to freak out about. Cause I don't want him to *do* anything with it after I say it. I don't need him to say it back. I don't need anything to *happen* afterward, I want to let him know where my head is at, so if he wonders why I stop and stare at him when he does something like watching, *completely* fascinated while I change my nose ring or waits without complaint while I choose a new color for my hair… he already *knows* why. He doesn't *have* to wonder.

… I'm even using *his* words now, repeating things he's said to me, twisting them for my own use. What's wrong with me."

"Aren't you supposed to end a question with a *question* mark, instead of a period?"

I nearly jumped out of my skin at the sound of Rashad's voice over my shoulder. My reflexive jolt made me knock over my can of San Pellegrino, and I groaned as bright, red-orange liquid spread across the counter.

Friggin' déjà vu.

I was writing an extremely personal blog post that would never see the light of day the *last* time I spilled one of those too.

228

This time though, I was writing from the office of Rashad's new studio space, in the building he shared with Raisa. Neither of them were open to customers, clients, or students yet, but I liked being here during the day, while they were working. Sometimes I helped, sometimes I did work of my own, and sometimes I made Rashad stop what he was doing to take pictures of my outfit so I could edit them for my blog. Because... I couldn't let what Drew did stop my flow.

One and a half weeks.

That's how long it had been since the appearance of those videos that turned my life upside down.

Two days.

That's how long it had been since Drew was arrested. Not for "revenge porn", which my lawyer and the police had told me would be a hard sell anyway, since the laws regarding that were still new, and underdeveloped. We buried him in all types of injunctions, and *that's* when, upon further investigation, we found that he had old, grainy videos dating back to our first times, filmed on his web cam. Back when I was a minor.

The police didn't take very kindly to Drew *and his mother*, who'd given him the idea in the first place — to release, not to film — possessing and intending to distribute pornography featuring a minor who hadn't given anything *near* consent. The inside of a jail cell is really, *really* good for teaching lessons. While they did the court thing, I would focus on continuing my brand.

Because... screw them.

"Are you reading over my shoulder, Rashad?" I asked as I quickly got out of my seat, using the napkins from my lunch to clean up the spill.

He shrugged. "Just that last line. Are you in here messing up these brand new floors?"

"Of *course* not." I finished drying up the spot, then stood. "See?"

"Yeah right," he chuckled. "I came to tell you some interesting news your homegirl Raisa dropped before she ran outta here to go meet Gabe."

"Hold on." I held up a hand as I picked up my phone from the table, mid-chime. "She actually just texted me."

"Girllll how about some NBA player invited Kieran to do an exclusive interview, LIVE TV, and as soon as Kieran opened his mouth, ole boy socked him in the face! Apparently, Kieran was screwing his wife! – Rai M."

My eyes went wide with shock as I read the message again, then looked up at Rashad. "Is this what you were gonna tell me, this stuff about Kieran?!"

He sucked his teeth. "Damn, y'all talk too much. I can't be the first to tell anything around here," he said, fake pouting. "But yeah… Cam fired his ass. Said she couldn't have the magazine associated with that kind of behavior."

"Yeah, you got scooped, buddy. Sorry," I giggled. "I never told you he called me *undateable*, did I? And basically tried to get me to sleep with him in the same conversation."

Rashad scowled. "Nah, you never told me that shit. Lucky for him, cause I would have punched his ass, like I socked Drew in the mouth."

Wait... what?

"You... *hit* Drew? When?!"

Rashad's eyes went wide, and he stood up, scratching his head. "Um... what I *meant* to say was... what had happened was... man, fuck him. Yeah, I punched him. And he deserved it."

I groaned, because I'd definitely asked Rashad *not* to touch Drew, but... I was secretly pleased. "Why did you put your hands on him? I'm *shocked* he didn't have you arrested. He's *that* kind of guy."

Rashad laughed. "Honestly... I'm shocked too. He probably knew his ass was already in hot water, though. But besides that... he deserved to get punched in the face, and I would do it again. I *should* have throat chopped his petty ass for messing with you."

"So...," I said, moving closer to him, and grabbing handfuls of his tee shirt to draw him against me. "You were defending me?"

"Absolutely."

"I like that."

"You *should*," he replied, giving me a sexy smirk before he lowered his lips to mine. "Hey... about that blog post..."

I sucked my teeth, pulling away so I could properly scold him. "So you *did* read it?"

He shrugged, and then his mouth spread into a sheepish grin. "Maaaaybe. I mean, you were sitting there, frozen, staring at the screen for like a full five minutes. I was watching you."

"Okay." I rolled my eyes, but somehow… I didn't mind that he read it. "So… what about it?"

Smiling, he sat down at the table, then pointed at the screen. "You *know* what this means right? We met… you didn't like me… we had *bomb* sex… and then… *Bianca caught feelings*," he said, in a teasing, singsong voice. "A particular, four letter, starts with an "L" type of feeling, to be specific. So… come on. You *know* what that means right? You *didn't* break my logic. You *proved* the point I made the first night we laid eyes on each other."

I crossed my arms over my chest, and tried to scowl, but I couldn't help the smile that overtook my face. "You… made a good point… *I guess.*" I shrugged, then pushed out a deep breath. "Okay. I, Bianca Bailey… will say it. Women are liars."

"*Yeeeahh,*" he said, grinning as he grabbed my hands to pull me between his open legs. "But that's aiight, B. You wanna know why?"

I leaned down, giving him a peck on the lips. "Why?"

"Cause I caught that same "L" word type of feeling. So… I guess men are liars too."

— the end —

If you enjoyed this book, please consider leaving a review at your retailer of choice. It doesn't have to be long - just a line or two about why you enjoyed the book, or even a simple star rating can be very helpful for any author!

Want to stay connected? Text 'CCJRomance' to 74121 or sign up for my newsletter. I'll keep you looped into what I'm doing!

Check out CCJROMANCE.COM for first access to all my new releases, signed paperbacks, merch, and more!

I'm all over the social mediasphere - find me everywhere @beingmrsjones

For a full listing of titles by Christina C Jones, visit www. beingmrsjones.com/books

about the author

Christina C. Jones is a best-selling romance novelist and
digital media creator. A timeless storyteller, she is lauded by
readers for her ability to seamlessly weave the complexities
of modern life into captivating tales of Black characters in
nearly every romance subgenre. In addition to her full-time
writing career, she co-founded Girl, Have You Read – a
popular digital platform that amplifies Black romance
authors and their stories. Christina has a passion for
making beautiful things, and be found crafting, cooking,
and designing and building a (literal) home with her
husband in her spare time.

Made in the USA
Middletown, DE
30 December 2024

68551641R00136